Finding Home

WITHIN THE CASTLE GATES BOOK FOUR

CANDEE FICK

Contents

Part One

Chapter One   2

Chapter Two   16

Chapter Three   29

Chapter Four   39

Chapter Five   48

Chapter Six   63

Chapter Seven   73

Chapter Eight   85

Part Two

Chapter Nine   98

Chapter Ten   112

Chapter Eleven   126

Chapter Twelve   137

Chapter Thirteen   150

Chapter Fourteen   160

Chapter Fifteen   172

Chapter Sixteen   186

Chapter Seventeen   198

Chapter Eighteen   208

Preview: Saving Grace   220

More Fiction   227

About Candee   229

Dedication

To all those who believe in fairy tales...
But don't feel like royalty.
This castle series is for you.

Become part of my family of readers and get a FREE novella plus access to exclusive bonus content. Sign up on my website at Can deeFick.com.

Part One

Chapter One

Today could be his last chance to explore for a while.

Nicholas Pennington tightened the cinch, then checked to see that his loaded hunting rifle was securely stowed. The valley was home to many a bird, but if he happened upon a deer in the dense woodlands, their cook would welcome the meat.

Turning on a booted heel, he led the gelding down the wide aisle of the stable.

Near the entrance, he caught a whine from an empty stall to his right and paused. A soothing whisper followed and Nicholas peered over the barrier.

"Easy now." Harold, their stable boy, knelt in the straw beside one of his father's prized hunting dogs. Based on her swollen belly and restless movements, they were likely to have pups before the day's end.

At least that would give his father something to be pleased about upon his expected return to Ravenglass from Whitehaven.

Harold glanced up with a grin. "Sneaking off again, are ye?"

"I don't have to sneak." Nicholas frowned. There was truth in his young friend's teasing. "However, if anyone should ask, I've gone in search of game and should return by early afternoon."

With a nod, the lad turned back to his task and Nicholas continued out into the stableyard before swinging up into the saddle. With a kick of his heels, he nudged his mount through the gate and turned away from the impressive castle his family had called home for hundreds of years.

Numerous additions and repairs had been made over the centuries and family lore stated there were Roman ruins at Muncaster's foundation. He found solace in knowing his family roots were buried in this beautiful land.

If only the Pennington name weren't such a burden.

At barely fifteen, Nicholas had yet to prove himself worthy of his heritage.

His father handled the role of landed gentry with ease and after being widowed years before, had diligently expanded their wealth by investing in merchant voyages. But while his father's attentions had turned to the sea, Nicholas preferred the rugged landscape of the Eskdale valley.

Craving the reassurance of the view, he rode up Muncaster Fell, then paused at the top to fully appreciate the sprawling landscape from the shimmering western sea beyond the village of Ravenglass, past the gray stone castle, and then eastward along the winding River Esk until the green valley gave way to the steeper terrain near Boot.

Suddenly eager to see the falls, he turned his mount to descend the hill and once on flat ground again, nudged the beast into a trot. Breathing deep of the clean air, he relaxed into the steady rhythm of hoofbeats muffled by the grasses along the path.

Six miles later, the open space had given way to thicker woods and the rush of water splashing over rocks grew steadily louder.

And above the faint pounding roar of the nearby falls, he caught the sound of singing. He slowed his approach and strained to make out the words.

"I've heard the lilting, at the yowe-milking, Lasses a-lilting before dawn o'day." The sweet female voice carried on the breeze and something about the sorrowful tone tugged at his heart.

The closer he got to the singer, the clearer the words became.

"But now they are moaning on ilka green loaning, the flowers of the forest are a' wede away." A slight hitch interrupted the last notes as if the singer were fighting tears.

Then again, who wanted to think about flowers withering away on such a fine day?

Nicholas rounded a rock outcropping and caught his first glimpse of the musician.

A girl of nearly ten years of age sat near the cliff's edge with a clear view of the plunging waterfall. Her reddish-brown hair fell in a tangled braid down her back, blending with the earth-tones of her homespun dress.

"The lasses are lonely and dowie and wae. Nae daffin', nae gabbin', but sighing and sobbing." The girl paused, then sniffed before wiping her cheeks on the sleeves of her dress.

"Why such a sad song?" Nicholas reined his horse to a halt nearby as the girl spun to face him with fearful eyes. He instantly recognized the daughter of Sir William Stanley and remembered passing by the knight's home, Dalegarth Hall, not long ago.

Did her family know she was out here alone?

He dismounted. "I'm Nicholas Pennington. I live over near—"

"Everyone knows who you are." She shrugged. "I've seen you hiking out here before. I'm Susannah."

"Well, Susannah, do you always serenade the falls?" He looped the reins over a branch, then lowered himself to the mist-drenched ground nearby.

Light sparkled in her green eyes. "Aye." The grin curving her pink lips faded. "But..."

"But?"

She sighed, her slight shoulders heaving. "Today is my mother's birthday and I miss her."

Of course. He recalled the fevers of last winter and the toll it took in their community. Her mother and younger brother had both perished along with a score of others in the valley.

He cleared his throat. "I lost my mother years ago and know the ache."

She turned to face the ravine. "She taught me that song from Scotland. Said 'twas a lament for the fallen." She took a deep breath and blew it out slowly as she wiped at the lingering tears on her face. "This was our favorite spot and so I came here to remember."

A companionable silence fell between them as he soaked in the refreshing view of water tumbling over the precipice into the pool below. Fresh water—like time—flowed on and yet like the rocky ravine, some things remained the same.

Like a child always missing their mother.

He peeked at the girl. "Will you teach me her song?"

Wide eyes turned his direction and pink blossomed in her pale cheeks before she looked away. Such sweet innocence should not have tasted grief.

"I've heard the lilting, at the yowe-milking..." Line by line, she sang the lyrics and waited for him to echo each phrase.

Wishing to cheer her, he harvested a pile of colorful wildflower blooms from among the lush rhododendrons and as the song unfolded, he wove the stems into a crown of flowers from the forest.

They too would eventually wither, but for a time, he prayed they would bring young Susannah joy.

Susannah glanced at the young man beside her and ignored the way his voice sometimes cracked with the melody. His long limbs seemed awkwardly thin but like her father's colt born that spring, he would likely grow into them. But with his thick brown hair, deep brown eyes, and easy smile, it was no wonder the village girls already whispered about him.

She had not been exaggerating to say that everyone knew Nicholas Pennington. And on the rare occasion her father drove them all the way to Ravenglass, she had been in awe of the majestic Muncaster Castle he called home.

What would it be like to live where her precious valley opened up to the sea?

Heat warmed her cheeks and she turned her attention to the last lines of the song. "Sighing and moaning, on ilka green loaning. The flowers of the forest are all wede away."

This time as he repeated the words, she sang along until the last notes lingered in the misty air. However, like her mother's laughter and love, they were swallowed up and washed away.

Beside her, Nicholas cleared his throat. "Thank you for allowing me to intrude upon your time of remembrance." He held out the stems he'd been weaving. "If I may, I'd like to offer these flowers to brighten your day."

She reached for the gift with a smile. "I wondered what you were doing with them."

He waved her aside. "Allow me." Leaning forward, he rested the circle atop her head, then winked. "I say, Susannah, you are as pretty as a princess."

Her blush grew even hotter and the blood rushing in her ears was louder than the nearby water falling onto the rocks.

"However, lass, if you are done with your serenade, I would see you safely home."

She glanced at the sun overhead. "Aye. My father will soon be looking for me." She rose to her feet and brushed the dirt from her skirt as Nicholas untied his horse.

The beast shook its head and shifted restlessly.

A rustle in the bushes behind them caught her attention and she turned in time to see a flash of red fur. Followed by a growl and a glimpse of snarling foamy fangs lunging toward her.

She jumped back an instant before Nicholas leaped in front of her. His bulk nudged her closer to the ravine and her boots slipped on the mist-dampened grass, sending her sprawling and dangling over the precipice.

As her hands scrambled for a hold on anything, she was vaguely aware of the desperate scuffle as Nicholas kicked the rabid fox away and reached for the gun hanging on his saddle.

Her toes landed on something solid and she pushed against it for leverage to stop her slide, only to have it give way. The now-un-supported earth beneath her belly collapsed and her weight carried her down the steep cliff, her body careening off the jagged surface and her left arm being sliced open by roots and rocks alike during her descent.

Her scream echoed in the ravine a moment before she landed on a narrow ledge cushioned only by a few plants.

The sound of a gunshot ricocheted above her and a few rocks fell onto her already-bruised body, trapping her upper body in place.

"Susannah!"

She whimpered, then opened her eyes to stare a long way up into Nicholas' horrified face as he leaned over the rim of the ravine.

"Oh, dear God. Don't move. I'll be right there."

Since even breathing hurt, there was little danger of movement. Tears blurred her vision.

A scuffling sound above drew her attention toward her right and soon Nicholas picked his way down the steep rocks. As he drew closer, she caught the heavy breathing of his exertion along with a whispered prayer that the ground would hold so she would not fall further.

The reminder of her precarious position on a ledge above the churning water below was followed by an intense wave of pain.

Another moan escaped her lips. Was she about to be reunited with her mother?

However, by the time Nicholas crouched beside her, the agony centered mostly on the left side of her body.

"I am so sorry. I didn't mean to push you over—"

"It wasn't you." She winced as he adjusted her hem over her bruised legs. "I'm the one who kicked away the earth while you were keeping me from getting bitten."

He leaned forward and removed the largest rock pinning her upper body. "We can debate that later, but first we need to get you—" He gasped as his dark eyes focused on her left arm.

She followed his gaze only to see her bloody flesh ripped open from elbow to wrist. Was that—?

Her stomach churned and she looked away quickly from the source of most of her pain

"Susannah. You're going to be fine." His voice held a strange conviction as he removed his jacket, followed by his shirt. He caught the fabric in his teeth and ripped it into strips. "I can't say the same for the fox."

She caught the twinkle in his eye. "Was it mad?"

"Completely." He wrapped a few strips tightly around her injured arm.

She shuddered to think what would have happened if she had contracted the illness herself. "Then you're my hero."

He grinned. "Never been called that before." His smile faded as he helped her to a sitting position and configured another piece of shirt fabric into a sling to secure her bandaged arm across her chest. "If it eases your mind, the animal did not seem to have ailed for long. In fact... How old are you?"

"Nine years. Ten this fall."

"Well, in a few years, you could make something from the pelt if you wished."

She welcomed the distraction from the pain. "A muff or collar for my cloak might be nice. What do you think?"

"A wise man leaves fashion decisions to the ladies." Another grin curved his lips before he turned his attention toward the cliff. "Now to get you above... I don't have a rope, but perhaps I could ride for—"

"No!" Her heart lurched and she grabbed his bare shoulder with her right hand. "Don't leave me alone."

His eyes widened. "You can't climb with only one arm and neither can I if I was to try to carry you. Unless you can hold yourself on my back, I see no way..." His voice trailed off as his gaze drifted from the remnants of his shirt to their escape route and back to her.

"Please?" Her voice broke as fresh tears welled in her eyes.

He sighed. "I must be as crazy as that fox to attempt this." He shook his head.

"I'm not that heavy and I promise I'll hold on tight and not wiggle." She sucked in a deep breath and forced a wobbly smile. Actually, with her injuries bandaged and secured, the pain was manageable.

Nicholas nodded, then donned his jacket again before tying the remaining strips of his shirt fabric into a longer rope.

Before long she was perched on his back with her legs around his waist. He had tucked the tails of his jacket up behind her as a bit of support and knotted the makeshift rope around them as a belt holding both her and the jacket tails in place.

He slowly stood and adjusted her weight, then repositioned her free hand's grip on the collar of his jacket. "This will have to do. Now, hold on tight with your legs and we'll be at the top before you know it."

She nodded, then buried her nose into his back as she tightened her grip. His chest expanded against her injured arm as he drew a deep breath and soon they were climbing.

Slowly.

But she appreciated his cautious approach even as her muscles began to quiver with the task of holding on. And yet, from her position on his back, she was aware of his wide shoulders and the effort it took to lift them both up the face of the cliff.

Dear God above, give him strength for the task.

Her feet only scraped against rocks twice before he heaved them over the edge and back onto level ground. Nicholas crawled forward a short distance before untying the knotted fabric to release their connection.

She climbed off his back and sat beside him as he heaved deep breaths from his exertion. He had not left her alone but rather gotten her to safety. "Thank you." Her voice quivered. "Now you're really my hero."

He chuckled, then rose to his feet. "Let's get you home." He helped her stand, then led the way to his horse.

"Don't forget my fox fur." She tried to smile, but as the reality of what she'd just survived began to sink in, her teeth chattered.

"I wouldn't dream of it." He put the carcass in a bag, then retrieved the wilting flower crown that had become dislodged when she'd begun to slide and replaced it on her head before lifting her to the saddle. A moment later, he had mounted behind her and spurred the horse into motion back down the trail.

Susannah was grateful for the strong arm anchored around her waist as tremors worked their way up her spine. She'd come too close to death and it would be a long time before she'd desire to return to her mother's favorite spot again.

Which reminded her...

She craned her neck to see him. "I'm ever so grateful you were there, but you never said why *you* were at the waterfall today."

A flash of pain in his dark brown eyes almost turned them black as he twisted his lips. "It was my last chance to explore for a while. My father is returning today from a trip for business and I'll be required at home. I'd much rather spend time out of doors but his idea of a proper education involves tutors and formal lessons. And many a lecture on what it means to be a Pennington. I fear I will never measure up to his expectations..."

She shook her head. "I believe you will excel at anything you put your mind to. That's what my father always said to my brother...before the fever robbed him of both wife and heir."

Tears blurred her vision once again. Dalegarth Hall was now a cold shell of her former home for she'd lost her father too in a different way. No longer affectionate or quick to laugh, he preferred a retreat to his study with a decanter of brandy over time spent with his surviving child.

Like the flowers she'd sung about, her bruised heart seemed to have likewise withered away.

She shivered, then huddled closer to the warmth of her new friend and rescuer as his arm tightened around her. If only she could stay in his circle of protection, but Nicholas had already turned off the path and approached the stone manor.

Her father stepped out of the barn. He lifted a hand in polite greeting, then halted, his eyes wide at the sight of her.

She glanced down at the blood-soaked bandages and her dirt-streaked dress. For certain, she looked like one who had come too close to the hereafter and with the reminder came a wave of pain.

"Susannah, my lily, whatever happened to you?"

Tears welled at the use of his affectionate nickname and she looked up to see him closing the distance as Nicholas spurred the horse forward. "I fell and—"

"Sir William, I came upon her near the falls and was about to escort her home when a rabid fox attacked. But in the chaos, she slipped over the edge."

"Dear God." Her father's face paled and she longed to reassure him.

"He saved me. Twice." Her voice hitched as she glanced up at her rescuer. "Once from the fox and again when he carried me up the cliff."

He met her gaze for a moment and swallowed hard before looking away. "I am sorry I could not prevent her from coming to harm." He reined the horse to a stop. "She will need stitching. Do you have—"

"Young man, it seems I have your bravery to thank for my lily's life."

A flash of emotion sparked in Nicholas' eyes and then was as quickly gone. After a simple nod, he lifted her from the saddle and carefully lowered her damaged body into her father's waiting arms.

Over an hour later, Nicholas turned his mount up Muncaster's gravel drive with a smile on his face and Susannah's song replaying in his mind.

When he'd set out that morning, he'd never imagined playing the role of hero nor receiving Sir William's praise. After all, there was a reason the man was a knight of the realm.

However, when Nicholas dismounted in the stable courtyard, his good mood evaporated at the sight of his father's carriage.

Harold rushed from the stone building, then stopped in his tracks with wide eyes scanning Nicholas' body.

He glanced down at his blood-streaked dirty garments and tugged his jacket together over his bare chest since his shirt had been transformed into bandages. He would need to make haste to be presentable before greeting his father or else their reunion would be marred by an even harsher lecture and punishment.

Nicholas stepped forward to hand off the horse, but halted when his father appeared in the doorway to the stable. He was too late to avoid discovery.

"Harold. Fetch the hot water." His father turned his stern frown from the retreating stable boy to Nicholas. "Now that he has deigned to return, my wayward son can care for his own horse." With that declaration, the man pivoted and disappeared inside.

Nicholas sighed as he trailed behind with one hand on the bridle. By the time he had removed the saddle and turned his horse into its stall, the boy had returned and activity centered around the first stall.

Resentment burned in Nicholas' chest as he watered his horse and rubbed a currycomb over the horse's withers.

Why would his father pay more attention to a laboring dog than the obvious blood on his only son's clothing? Blood that could have been his own and not that of a young girl?

"I have your bravery to thank for my lily's life."

The memory of Sir William's words soothed the sting of his father's hasty judgment. At least someone recognized his worth.

"He saved me. Twice."

Make that two people who looked favorably upon him.

A smile curved his lips at the memory of the hero-worship in young Susannah's eyes. Even at fifteen years of age, what lad didn't enjoy the attentions of a lass?

And yet, if he had not been out riding that morning, she would have faced the fox alone with far direr consequences.

His tasks done, Nicholas strode toward the exit, then paused by the first stall. "Harold? Where is the stablemaster? I need to warn him of the presence of rabid animals in—"

His father's bark of laughter silenced his report. "Where would *you* see a rabid anything? The only madness I see—"

"I shot such a beast not two hours ago near Dalegarth Falls." Nicholas stared at his father. "During my ride along the Esk, I came upon a girl mourning her mother." He quickly relayed the events of the morning including the fox's attack, the cliff rescue, and his delayed return after fetching a physician from the closest village to tend to the girl's injuries. "I left the animal's carcass with her father if you require proof. I thought the pelt would make a nice muff or collar when she grows."

By the end of the tale, Harold seemed eager for more details, but Nicholas' father only sneered. "If you had to rescue a lass, you should have picked a worthy one, not a common waif."

"Since when is Sir William's daughter considered unworthy or a commoner?" Nicholas folded his arms over his bare chest and glared. "But no matter her lineage, she's a brave child. She cried more today over her mother's death than her injuries. Wait a few years, I've no doubt she'll be the village darling."

With her coloring and sweet singing voice, suitors would be lining up in years to come and perhaps Nicholas would count himself among them.

"It wouldn't take much for her to stand out in puny Boot." His father rolled his eyes. "I've never understood why Sir William would be content with the income from his tenant farmers when there is greater wealth to be found on the seas and in commerce."

Nicholas clenched his jaw and remained silent. There was no reasoning with his father, especially when the man cast a disdainful look at Nicholas' disheveled attire.

"You will never be worthy if you continue like this. It's time you understood where our wealth truly comes from and prove yourself a true Pennington. I was going to tell you over dinner but I've arranged for you to join the crew of the Swan as an ordinary seaman."

"But I know nothing of—"

"Exactly. However, once you understand sailing, you will be able to assist in the planning of future voyages along the trade routes."

Trade routes that might not exist in the next ten years. But Nicholas knew better than to remind his father that since Britain had just declared war on France and enforced a naval blockade, such seafaring journeys might be curtailed in the future.

"We are leaving in the morning for Whitehaven. I will make the introductions and see you off. Now, go. Rid yourself of your filth and have your valet pack your belongings." His father then crouched to pat the head of the dog, effectively dismissing his son.

Nicholas nodded at the wide-eyed Harold, then turned to trudge along the lane toward the castle.

He already missed his home and the picturesque Esk valley, but could not deny the inner tug toward the looming challenge. How long would it take to learn the seafaring trade? Could he make his father proud?

I believe you will excel at anything you put your mind to.

The memory of Susannah's sweet words lifted his spirits.

If he dedicated himself to learning everything he could on the journey, within a year, he'd be back home and have regained his father's approval.

Chapter Two

~Three years later

G ravel crunched under the wheels of the carriage as they slowly approached Muncaster and Susannah could not help but
squirm on the squabs as she peeked out the window at the line of
other carriages with various footmen assisting other guests.

She never imagined she would ever be invited to a celebration at
the impressive castle.

Actually, her father had received the initial invitation. She
glanced across to the man who watched her with an indulgent
smile and grinned in return.

It wasn't every day that a man was elevated to baronet by the
King. Or a common occurrence for a girl to perform in the presence of the Duke of Middlesbrough.

When their local vicar, Reverend Brooks, had asked her to sing
in honor of the fallen as part of the ceremony, she'd been surprised
and then terrified. Her father said the choice was a tribute to him
as well and therefore she wished nothing more than to be worthy
of the moment.

Her midsection fluttered with constrained nerves and she smoothed a hand over the green silk of her new gown.

In honor of the occasion—and because her other options were either too ordinary or too small as her body changed almost overnight—they had traveled north to Carlile and commissioned a dressmaker.

Although now she felt like an impostor playing dress-up in her mother's clothes. But the dressmaker said the color matched her eyes and complemented the reddish hues in her brown hair.

"You look lovely, my dear." Her father's smile turned nostalgic.

Of course, over the past few weeks, he had alternated between grumbling that he knew nothing of women's fashion and more contemplative moments when he'd wished she had a proper woman's influence in her life. To the point she feared he might do something rash like remarry before his heart was ready simply to give her a mother.

Their carriage rolled to a stop and she tugged on the long gloves that concealed the unsightly red scar on her arm. In the midst of her public singing, fashion's dictates would shield her from the scrutiny of those who did not know the story.

The story of a day she still held close to her heart and revisited in her memories often.

The day a handsome boy saved her life. Twice.

She could only imagine what Nicholas looked like now...

What would he think of her? Would he remember her as anything other than a bruised and bloody child? Whereas she still recalled in vivid detail the strength of his back as he carried her up the cliff and the warmth of his hold while they were on horseback.

The carriage door opened and a footman lowered the steps. Her father exited first, then turned to help her down.

In addition to his cliff-side heroics, Nicholas had somehow also resurrected her relationship with her father. For after her near brush with death, he abandoned his brandy and Dalegarth Hall was now a home again.

Once again she was her father's precious Lily.

If only she could thank Nicholas, but she'd never gotten another chance.

On her father's arm, they made their way up the cobblestone path to the wide doors where they were greeted by a liveried butler with a kindly twinkle in his eye. A footman stepped forward to direct them through the opulent entryway to a large drawing room already teeming with bejeweled women and formally dressed gentlemen.

Since the common folk of Ravenglass would not have been invited to such a gathering in favor of the elite members of the peerage or wealthy merchants, she recognized few faces. However, her father moved among the other guests with ease.

How could she have forgotten he was a Knight and that until today's ceremony had been of higher rank than the owner of this very castle? Yet somehow he mingled as easily here in a castle as in the fields around their village.

There was some truth to Shakespeare's admonition of to thine own self be true.

However, even as she properly acknowledged her father's introductions and adhered to the manners her mother had taught, a part of her soul longed for nothing more than to be out of doors among God's beauty. To be surrounded by flowers with the sun on her face rather than suffocated by cloying perfumes.

Thankfully, an announcement was made and along with the other guests, they moved to claim chairs facing the fireplace. Mr. Pennington—soon to be Sir Thomas—was seated in a large chair at the front.

Within minutes, the elegant Duke of Middlesbrough strode through their midst to the front. Despite his country seat being located a far distance to their east near the North Sea, he was the closest they had to nobility living as they did in the very north of England.

"On behalf of the Pennington family, I welcome you to Muncaster Castle for this special occasion." The middle-aged duke offered an easy smile and a nod at their host. "I am well pleased to also relay our King's personal greetings direct from London."

A slight murmur arose from the assembly, but whether in awe due to the source over 250 miles to the south or concern over rumors of their sovereign's decline, she could not say.

"We are here to honor the achievements of two men with the bestowing of one title." The duke positioned his hands behind his back and first recounted Mr. Pennington's extensive contributions to the general economy and shipping advancements that had benefited both the region as well as the national military efforts.

All Susannah knew of the man's business dealings were tales of numerous trips away from home while Nicholas was burdened with tutors and high expectations that he be worthy of the family name.

While the man's hair and eye color matched that of his son, their attitudes were markedly different for the current honoree soaked in the praise with a smug expression as if today's ceremony was a foregone conclusion.

The duke ended his accounting with a chuckle. "But perhaps Mr. Pennington's greatest achievement is that of siring such a fine son and then sending him to sea."

The man in question winced, then let out an awkward chuckle.

Her face heated at the memory of her childish crush and the devastating sting of rejection when the handsome young man had never returned to visit her during her recovery. It was only months later that she learned Nicholas had sailed away the next morn apparently at his father's order.

"After a year at sea, it is my understanding that the young Mr. Pennington was then impressed into our Royal Navy where he served gallantly during the Battle of Trafalgar late last year and helped prevent the invasion of our homeland." The duke paused as a burst of applause spattered around the room. "And in the Battle of San Domingo this February, his heroic actions saved the lives of his captain and numerous fellow seamen. His actions were reported to the King and brought additional attention to his family. Mr. Nicholas Pennington will be promoted in the field immediately, but it was decided that he should also be rewarded with an inherited title."

If only Nicholas were here to know what was said of him and relay the story himself.

And yet she was not surprised to hear of the man he was becoming. After all, a half hour on the side of a cliff had convinced her of his potential for greatness even at the age of fifteen.

The duke reached inside his jacket and retrieved a rolled parchment. Once unfurled, he read the formal decree of the King creating and bestowing the hereditary title of baronet upon the Pennington line with the additional benefit of conferring the rank of Knight upon the son when he reached his twenty-first year.

"Henceforth, Mr. Thomas Pennington, you shall be known as Sir Thomas." The duke placed the parchment upon a small table nearby and extended a hand. "Let me be the first to congratulate you, Sir Thomas."

The new baronet rose and shook hands with the duke. "Thank you, your grace."

Deafening applause filled the room and Sir Thomas' simple nod to those assembled did little to dampen his smile or quiet their cheers.

After several minutes, the duke raised his hands for quiet before continuing. "In light of the events that precipitated the honor, I would ask that we set aside a few minutes to pay tribute to those countrymen who have fallen in the war. Reverend Brooks?" The duke nodded toward one side of the room and their vicar hurried to join him.

"All rise and let us pray."

As the vicar led them in prayers for the fallen and a speedy resolution to the conflict on the continent, Susannah pressed a hand over the renewed flutters in her midsection and hummed softly to loosen her vocal cords.

Surely God would understand her distraction?

"And now, if you will all be seated, I have asked Miss Stanley to sing a memorial lament borrowed from our neighbors to the north. Miss Stanley?" The vicar gestured for her to take up position between the Duke of Middlesbrough and the new baronet of Muncaster Castle.

She walked on shaky legs to the designated spot and turned to face the crowd. Never had she sung before so many, and yet as she glanced at her father for encouragement, she felt his love and answered with a smile.

She closed her eyes in order to envision the waterfall and the fading memory of her mother. After a deep breath, the words flowed from her lips.

"I've heard the lilting, at the yowe-milking, Lasses a-lilting before dawn o' day; But now they are moaning on ilka green loaning; The Flowers of the Forest are a' wede away..."

When the last note lingered in the room, she opened her eyes to find many ladies dabbing handkerchiefs beneath their eyes.

Beside her, the duke cleared his throat. "Thank you. That was beautifully done."

She glanced up to see brimming tears, but it would never do to notice. She bobbed into a quick curtsy, then returned to her father's side as the butler announced from the doorway that refreshments were being served in the dining room.

As a line formed to congratulate the new baronet, happily her father steered her toward the punch bowl for her mouth was dry.

However, along the way, they were stopped frequently by those wishing to complement her on her singing...and praise her father for having such a daughter.

Was Sir Thomas fielding similar sentiments about his offspring?

Eventually the crowd thinned out and they were able to approach Sir Thomas. Upon introduction, she dipped into another curtsy and murmured the proper greeting.

Sir Thomas nodded. "Thank you for the lovely song. You must be the child my son rescued from a rabid fox."

"I am." Her eyes widened in surprise. "It's a bit warm today for such a thing, but I sewed the pelt into the hood of my winter cloak..." Heat flooded her face at being caught talking of clothing in front the baronet.

Her father chuckled at her exuberance.

Thankfully, Sir Thomas merely smiled. "Nicholas spoke highly of you that day and I can see he was correct in his predictions." The man's gaze swept over her gown then came to rest on her hair.

Predictions? Of her singing...or something else?

She fought the urge to squirm and deflected the conversation. "Your son is the only one who did anything noteworthy that day."

Her father rested a hand on her back. "She has grown much since then and has made me very proud. Now that she is almost thirteen and practically turning into a woman before my eyes, I am reminded how quickly life can change." He cleared his throat. "I would like to see my Lily's future secured." He forced a laugh as if trying to sound casually convincing.

"Indeed. Our legacy lives on through our children." A gleam of interest appeared in Sir Thomas' eye. "And impacts our region. Perhaps we should discuss such things at a later date."

"Agreed." Her father smiled as if relieved, but before she could decipher his meaning, another well-wisher intruded and the moment was lost.

Nicholas secured the ammunition chest and checked to see their supply of powder bags and wadding was protected from the elements. After the ordinary seamen swabbed the boards, it was his responsibility to see the gunnery supplies on the upper deck were undisturbed and ready at a moment's notice.

Not that there had been many skirmishes in the last six months as the HMS Superb helped patrol the Spanish coast with their seventy-four cannons.

Before moving on to the next gun, he braced his feet on the rocking deck and drew in a deep breath of the sea-scented air that always reminded him of Ravenglass. The sails overhead snapped in the breeze, their ropes and wooden pulleys creaking with the ship's movement and calling him upward to explore the rigging.

When aloft, he could pretend the views were those from a castle turret or Muncaster Fell. That the shoreline glimpses of France or Spain were of his beloved Esk valley leading to a paradise of rhododendrons and waterfalls.

It had been three very long years away from home and none of it by his choice.

First, his father had shackled him to the Swan. Then after a long year of delays and changes in plans, he was a week from home on an inbound voyage when a press gang boarded their vessel. At the age of sixteen, he'd found himself an unwilling member of the Royal Navy and assigned to a gunnery crew to serve his country in the battle against Napoleon.

Being robbed of his choices still left a bitter taste in his mouth. However, he had to admit that two years later, the continued physical activity onboard a ship had yielded muscles on his frame.

And if his trouser legs told the truth, he had even grown another inch or two in height.

"Nick, my boy."

He turned to see the official blue coat of the Gunner in charge of all the armaments. Was he about to be scolded for loitering in his tasks?

"Captain Drake wishes to see us immediately."

"Yes, sir." One thing he had learned in the Royal Navy was that orders were to be obeyed without question.

As he followed behind his superior, Nicholas worried that he might have been errant in his duties. Or had there been distressing news from home?

When they slipped inside, the wardroom had been turned into a strategy meeting with a map of the coastline and various lists spread upon the table. All of the highest-ranking naval officers were present, including the fleet commander and a few other captains who must have ferried over from another ship.

Captain Drake nodded at their arrival, then turned his attention back to the admiral.

"A year ago, at Trafalgar, we prevented the invasion of Britain. And since our victory at San Domingo in February, we have ruled the seas. Not only have we not engaged in open water battles, but with our patrols, we have prevented the enemy from regaining support and cut off their supplies." The admiral paused as the others gave a rousing cheer. "And now Wellington has requested our assistance with more than moving his troops and supplies."

The resulting barrage of questions was silenced by the admiral's upraised hands. "We are to supplement his artillery with our cannons. On land." Despite another murmur of voices, the fleet's commander continued. "I am allocating two nine-pounders from the quarterdecks as well as a sufficient gunnery crew from each ship in the fleet to fulfill my obligation."

The admiral went on to explain the details of the operation including communication and supplies while Nicholas contemplated the wisdom of such a decision.

Unlike the massive twenty-four pounders found behind most of the gun ports, the smaller guns would be easier to transport on land and faster to load since the powder and shell were joined into a fixed round.

However, had his presence been requested because he was about to venture ashore to engage the enemy there?

A few minutes later, the admiral dismissed the visiting captains, then turned to their captain. "Did you send for Mr. Pennington?"

Captain Drake pointed to their quiet corner of the room. "He is there."

The admiral strode closer. "Your captain has spoken highly of you after the Battle of San Domingo. Seems you're something of a hero in this crew and our King and the War Department both agree."

"Thank you, sir." He dipped his head in respect even as he recalled the incident.

In the middle of the battle, enemy fire had hit the middle mast and loosened the main sail, sending a corner drooping to the deck. Without the ability to properly harness the wind, they had drifted sideways taking their cannons out of range and exposing their flank to the enemy guns.

Nicholas had seen a need and responded on instinct. Leaving behind his post resupplying powder bags to the top deck guns, he had grabbed the corner of the heavy canvas, secured it around his waist with a length of rope as a belt, then used both hands to scale the rigging.

Like the day he'd once climbed a cliff with a wounded waif of a child tied onto his back, he had ignored the possibility of failure and the smoke and explosions and a near miss by another cannon shell. Once near the damaged section of wood, he was able to use the remnants of rope there plus his substitute belt to secure the corner of the sail. The wind quickly caught the fabric, almost ripping it out of his hands and tossing him into the sea, but somehow he was able to hold on.

And by the time he had returned to the deck, the Superb was back on course and engaged in the battle once more.

The admiral smiled. "You are to be rewarded as well as commended for your heroic actions."

"Thank you, sir." What else could he say?

Thankfully, the admiral immediately departed and he was spared another awkward reply.

But not before Captain Drake noticed his discomfiture and chuckled. "He wished to meet you in person. Now, as for the admiral's orders, Gunner Clarke I would like you to assemble two crews for shore duty and bring me their names. They can be on a rotation basis or permanent assignment per your discretion but with competent leadership that does not include our Mr. Pennington."

Nicholas' raised his eyebrows. "Sir?"

The captain turned to the table and began sorting through a few papers searching for something. "You are being promoted to Gunner's Mate at petty officer grade to train newly impressed seamen to man the guns."

Nicholas blinked as Gunner Clarke clapped him on the shoulder.

A promotion? Would he be given a blue coat as well? The additional responsibility was humbling, but mostly he felt relief not to be assigned to the shore duty.

After all, in the course of offering troop transport for Wellington, most onboard had already seen the bloody hospital evacuations and those dying of disease. Ship fare might be bland but he was safer here.

Captain Drake finally located whatever he'd been looking for and with a secretive smile held out a folded letter to Nicholas. "You've a message from home. And should we still be engaged in this conflict, I'm looking forward to doing the honor when the time comes."

The honor?

Nicholas could hardly keep up with the number of surprises his morning had held.

"In the meantime, you may have a few minutes of privacy to read it, then report to Gunner Clarke for a further explanation of your new duties." Their captain waved both men toward the door. "You are dismissed."

A few minutes later, Nicholas found a quiet spot near the rear of the ship and opened the sealed parchment. His eyes burned at the welcome sight of his father's handwriting before he noticed the date.

June. Two months ago. But getting ordinary mail to the various ships roaming along the coast often involved waiting for a military dispatch to be delivered from headquarters along with a bag of assorted other collected mail.

His eyes took in the news from home that his father had been styled as a baronet. And as his heir, Nicholas was to be knighted on his twenty-first birthday. If the war continued that long, his commanding officer would see to the ceremony.

He chuckled. When the admiral and his captain talked of commendations and honors, they were not exaggerating.

In another three years, he would be Sir Nicholas.

While his father was already Sir Thomas...

Some changes were hard to comprehend and yet his chest tightened at the thought he had brought permanent honor to the Pennington name. Was his father finally proud?

Nicholas turned his attention to the remainder of the letter.

In light of your new position, I have arranged a marriage to the Stanley girl when you are both of age. She is turning out to be quite the beauty...

He should be offended at his lack of choice in the matter, and yet he had thought of her often over the years.

While he tried to imagine her appearance now as she approached womanhood, mostly he recalled Susannah's sweet voice, memorable lyrics, and her bravery. How she had called him her hero. But mostly her belief that he could excel in whatever he pursued.

Hopefully her injury had not left her with too much of a scar for her sake. He had accumulated a few of his own lately and knew women were particular about such things.

Would she think him much changed and for the better?

Nicholas tucked the missive safely away in his shirt and vowed to write her a letter later now that he had the right as her betrothed.

His smile grew.

It had been quite an eventful day with a naval promotion, the promise of knighthood, plus a future as a baronet with a lovely wife by his side.

All of which provided something new for him to pursue with excellence.

Chapter Three

S usannah stared out the window at the driving rain splashing into the puddles on the path to their front door, willing her father to appear at any moment.

And not just because they were waiting dinner.

"Where can he be?" Her stepmother's voice from the dining room bristled with rising irritation.

"What did you expect moving us to the middle of nowhere?" A high-pitched whine punctuated the question, reinforcing Susannah's reasons for lingering in the parlor apart from the others. "At least in town there are civilized streets for when it rains."

Susannah closed her eyes and prayed once again for patience, for months of experience had taught her that Susan, her elder-by-a-few-months stepsister, would never forgive her mother's choice in marrying a country gentleman. The girl had her ambitions set on bigger towns south of Cumbria's Lake District.

"Why do we have to wait? I'm hungry now." Of course, Prudence was concerned about the food.

"Hush. You could stand to skip a meal else I need to let out your dresses again."

Susannah winced.

Her early impressions of a nurturing mother had been quickly supplanted. For as the woman adjusted to her local status as a knight's wife, the new Lady Stanley began to complain about her husband's rambling about the countryside and tracking mud onto the carpets.

If only she hadn't needed new gowns, her father would never have met Mrs. Thorne.

But after their initial visit to Carlile for a dress for the baronet's ceremony, they'd returned twice more for a fall and a spring wardrobe. Her father then decided to court the widowed dressmaker and soon thereafter tied the knot just five months before.

While it was strange indeed to have the former shopkeeper as a mother figure, the woman's skill with a needle was helpful as Susannah grew and at barely fifteen developed more womanly curves.

However, simultaneously acquiring two sisters near her age had been a monumental adjustment.

At least her father still called her his lily and invited her along on exploratory jaunts through the countryside. Times he often used to encourage her to do her best to keep the peace at home.

She sighed.

The only place she ever found true peace now was out of doors. There were simply too many opinions to consider inside these walls.

"Susannah, dear?"

She turned from her vigil at the window and found Mrs. Warren, their part-time day help, draping her woolen shawl above her head. "You won't consider staying until the storm passes?"

"Nay." The woman smiled. "I wilna melt and me family needs me to home."

"Take care." Moments later Susannah watched the woman dash down the path toward Boot. A shiver ran up her spine to think that her father was somewhere out there in the deluge.

"Did the maid leave?" Lady Stanley's strident voice carried throughout the main floor. "I have a list of chores that need her attention."

As if none of the other women in the household were capable of cleaning.

But no, the new Lady Stanley wanted to hire more servants. While her economical father preferred a simpler lifestyle.

Somehow a single gown for the Muncaster Castle event paired with his title gave Mrs. Thorne a more affluent expectation for her marriage. Of course, Susannah knew they had income enough for their needs—and perhaps another servant if truly required—but the money could just as easily be saved for the future or used to help another in need.

Someday when she was the mistress of a household, she vowed to be frugal so as not to burden her husband with unnecessary expenses. A smile curved her lips. Assuming her father's agreement with Sir Thomas stood the test of time, she would eventually take that role at Muncaster Castle.

It was both strange but somewhat reassuring to already be betrothed at her age, and yet Nicholas would make a fine husband. If his character had not changed during his five years at sea.

She might have worried that he would reject her, except his letter accepting their fathers' arrangement was hidden upstairs in her box of treasures. Since it was all set in motion before her stepmother and sisters invaded Dalegarth Hall, she was relieved to still have something to call her own. There was nothing to stop her eventual marriage.

Assuming Nicholas survived the war.

Another chill of foreboding skittered over her skin and sank into her bones.

If the ache in her chest was any indication, something was deadly wrong.

Susannah rushed to the dining room. "You should eat before the food goes to waste. I am going out to look for Father." Ignoring the trio of startled faces, she paused just long enough to snatch her woolen cloak from a hook in the entry way and then stepped out into the storm.

Oh, why had she not thought of it earlier?

Today was the anniversary of her father's wedding to her mother and there was only one place he felt comfortable reminiscing now that he had remarried. As much as she wished to rail at him for making them worry, she understood the need for private reflection.

But as she bent her hooded head into the wind and hurried down the muddy trail toward the falls, she knew he would never linger in such weather without cause. Especially with darkness fast approaching.

She should have thought to bring a lantern but it was too late to turn back now.

Fear drove her feet onward until she came around a bend and her path was blocked by a body lying on the ground.

A man wearing her father's great coat.

She surged forward and fell to her knees beside him. "Papa!" Shaking his shoulders, her mind scrambled to make sense of it all. For not only were his eyes open and staring up into the rain, his limbs were stiff and unresponsive.

"No! No...No..." A sob caught in her throat.

What had caused such an accident? She glanced around the darkening terrain, taking in the furrowed lines uphill and the jagged rock nestled in a bed of lush foliage near his head. An irregularly shaped gash marred his temple near his hairline but the rain must have washed away the blood.

Blood that would have yet flowed were he alive. Meaning he had been gone long before she thought to come looking.

She raised her face into the harsh winds and screamed, tears mixing with the icy rain that soaked her dress as sobs shook her chest.

Why did one of her favorite places in the world have to be tainted with such a tragedy?

Sometime later, both numbed by the harsh weather and the crushing sorrow, she staggered to her feet and turned to fetch the local blacksmith.

She could not leave her father in the storm.

A moan escaped her lips, followed by a whispered melody. "But now they are moaning on ilka green loaning; the Flowers of the Forest are a' wede away..."

Days later, her silent lament still rose as she stood by the graveside outside St. Catherine's church. And not just at the loss of her father but also her home.

Once Reverend Brooks concluded the service, she shuffled along with the other mourners toward Dalegarth Hall for the funeral dinner. Despite her dulled senses, their whispers of gossip bludgeoned her already bruised heart.

For since Sir William Stanley had died without a male heir, the family property of Dalegarth Hall was entailed to a distant cousin she had not seen in over a decade. At least in his will, her father had bequeathed a large sum to her stepmother for them to live on.

Except Lady Stanley—too proud to return to Carlile where she'd been known as a dressmaker—was moving their family south to Liverpool so her daughters could find suitable matches.

Once back inside her childhood home, Susannah succumbed to the pressures of the village busybodies and prepared a small plate to nibble on before finding a chair in the corner.

However, she was not allowed a moment's peace before her stepsisters joined her at their mother's order to cheer her up. Except their superficial chatter tested her endurance.

As time passed in agonizing slowness, various people intruded on her refuge to extend their condolences. While most were from Boot, there were a few from Ravenglass including Muncaster's aging steward who paid his respects from Sir Thomas who was in the south of England on government business.

After most of the visitors were gone, Susannah slipped upstairs to her room to pack her trunk uninterrupted.

First inside was the simple wooden box containing the salvaged bits of fox fur from her old cloak, her mother's locket on a gold chain, one of her brother's wooden blocks, and Nicholas' letter. And just yesterday, she had added one of her father's handkerchiefs and the copy of their betrothal agreement that she'd stolen from her father's study before it could be misplaced by the new heir or destroyed by her stepmother.

All symbols of those she loved in the past and those she hoped to love in the future.

She added a layer of summer dresses to conceal her treasures, then looked around her room for other reminders of home to carry her through the lonely years ahead. A framed portrait of her parents and her father's Bible found their way into the trunk between additional layers of clothing.

Her faith and memories were all she had from her past, but there was still a future, wasn't there? Wouldn't she someday return to this region as a bride?

She brushed a tear from her cheek.

Once they were settled in Liverpool, she would write to both Sir Thomas and Nicholas.

~Spring 1809

"How dare you presume to ask my manservant to post a letter?" Lady Stanley fanned her reddened face with the folded parchment as she paced the drawing room.

Susannah blinked back tears and bowed her head over her embroidery. Before the intrusion, she had been quietly stitching a row of lilac-colored flowers onto the border of a handkerchief.

It had been six months since their arrival in Liverpool and she had simply tried to update Sir Thomas about her situation and inquire about Nicholas' wellbeing.

But never could she have guessed that Duncan would betray her trust.

"Not only is it unseemly to write to a man above your station, who is this Nicholas to you?"

Susannah lifted her head to see that her stepmother had opened the letter and perused the contents. Had the woman no shame?

Angry tears stung her eyes. "He is a childhood acquaintance currently serving in the Royal Navy."

That much was true, but if she'd had to ask, perhaps Lady Stanley did not know the full truth. Perhaps in their short marriage and because of her own youth, her father had never confided in his new wife?

Something warned her to exercise caution with the topic of Nicholas, but thankfully the woman seemed appeased by her explanation.

"I know you miss your life there, but this is your new home and things are different now. Not only do proper ladies not write letters to unmarried men, but it's an unnecessary expense."

Susannah had to bite her tongue to keep from pointing out that Pru's perpetual boxes of sweets and Susan's collection of fans and fripperies cost more than the simple postage of a single letter.

Not to mention that her stepmother had spent the bulk of her newfound wealth to purchase this house in what she considered a proper part of town.

Then again, in Susannah's opinion, nowhere in crowded Liverpool was deserving of such a label. The only benefit she could find was they were further from the dangerous docks that reeked of whale oil and rotten fish...and a few of the houses had private kitchen gardens that only teased with reminders of living things.

Lady Stanley's lecture continued with a tirade about how frugality needed to be exercised with her widow's inheritance in order to secure dowries for her daughters. And why they all needed to help with the household tasks in order to get by with only two servants.

However, Susannah already did most of their shared tasks in exchange for a room to herself on the third floor instead of sharing with slovenly Pru.

Her stepmother waved the stolen letter one last time before tossing it in the fire. "In order to teach you a lesson, Anna, you will be responsible for baking all of the bread for the next week instead of our purchasing it at the market. Starting now."

"Yes, ma'am." Fighting tears at the injustice, she set aside her stitching and exited the room.

Oh, how she hated the name Anna.

It had all started innocently enough when Lady Stanley had been introducing the girls to a neighbor as Susan, Susannah, and Pru...and a slip of the tongue reduced her to Anna.

A mistake that quickly became a deliberate way to avoid any confusion between the girls.

Just like that, her identity had been whittled away. All in the name of keeping the peace like her father would have wanted.

But now she had been banished once again to the kitchen as punishment.

When they first moved to Liverpool, Susannah had been unable to sleep for her grief and her stepmother had been more than willing to provide a list of tasks to keep her busy to the point of exhaustion.

Now that the edge of loss held less sting, she had work-worn hands, kitchen skills, and sometimes even the urge to take her frustrations out on a lump of dough.

She entered the kitchen to find it empty and assumed Lucy, their general maid and housekeeper, was occupied with the laundry. Perhaps once the loaves were rising, she could help the woman begin work on the evening meal.

Anything to avoid spending time around Lady Stanley or her daughters while still furious over the sight of her burned letter.

After donning an apron over her dark gray mourning dress, she gathered the ingredients and settled into her task of stirring the dough. Soon, she began to hum a melody and smiled at the lingering influence of her mother's memory. Today's song was a peaceful hymn for a change.

Her stepmother once heard her singing her mother's lament and complained it was too morose. Ever since, she bade Susannah to sing livelier tunes around their new friends whenever they entertained guests...

Having been married for less than a year, the trio of mother and daughters had exited their proper mourning much earlier than Susannah would. They had inserted themselves into the whirl of Liverpool's social hierarchy while leaving the orphan to find her own quiet entertainment.

Susannah turned the dough out onto the flour-dusted table and began to knead it with steady movements.

She might have enjoyed walks in a park but rarely had time. Not to mention that on her first visit, she had been unimpressed by the lack of creativity or variety of flowers. Then again, nothing could compare to her home valley and the mountains of the Lake District.

If God spared Nicholas' life during the war, she would have the best of reasons to return home.

Eventually.

But in the meantime, she was only fifteen with much still to learn about running a household as a proper wife.

Chapter Four

~June 1812

Nicholas propped his hands on his hips as he supervised the unloading of more ammunition from the rowboat.

The six years since his initial promotion had been a never-ending cycle of voyages in support of Wellington's forces along the Spanish coast. Navy ships navigated the sometimes-rough seas to land both troops and supplies before taking the wounded away in addition to carrying the post and dispatches.

The HMS Superb and others in the fleet sometimes patrolled the rivers to maintain a clear line of retreat if necessary, but more recently had begun raiding the French coast to destroy Napoleon's outposts and weaken those garrisons.

Nicholas had been there for it all from the evacuation of Corunna to the raid at Santona harbor. However, with the loss of yet another gunnery crew and cannon, he had been assigned to lead the shore-excursions.

While twenty-four was young for an officer, he had labored alongside most of his current crew for years, thereby earning their respect as one who did not rest on his rank or title.

Benjamin hoisted a crate upon his brawny shoulders. "Where are we headed this time?"

Nicholas watched as Owen hurried to help steady the load and lower it safely into the waiting wagon. "We're to support Popham's march on the port of Santander."

Percy laughed on his way back for another crate. "God willing, he will succeed for it would be a welcome change to have the Superb docked in a real harbor with a road."

"As opposed to coordinating a delivery with a rowboat to a rough coastal beach?" Nicholas smiled, then nodded at the ship's crew who obviously agreed as they transferred the last crate from their boat and prepared to shove off.

"Not just us, but all of Wellington's supply chain would benefit, especially as we push the French further north and eventually out of Spain." Relative newcomer John worked with lanky Miles to organize the loaded crates and make room for the last few. "The Prince Regent taking over for the King last year seemed to have spurred them to progress at last..."

Nicholas cocked his head at the man's sharp assessment of the political changes and military maneuvers. He did not know much of John's history. Only that he had enlisted—unlike those who had been impressed or bought a commission—and that he was from the Yorkshire region—unlike the others who had grown up by the sea.

And that they had already been mistaken for each other once from behind since they were of similar height and coloring. Although Benjamin was quick to mention that Nicholas' easy smile was a dead giveaway from the front...

"If that is all, Sir Nicholas?"

Pulled from his musings, Nicholas turned to the men already taking their place at the oars to return to the Superb. "Thank you and I wish you safe journey back to ship." He motioned to the wagon where Miles was rearranging their semaphore communication flags to make room for the last crate. "Tell Captain Drake to watch for a signal fire three nights from now. We should be a few miles up the coast by then."

With a nod of acknowledgment, the men leaned into the oars and set to sea, stroking hard to get past the breaking waves. Nicholas watched long enough to see them past the worst of the rocks before rejoining his crew who already had the loaded wagon moving slowly inland to rejoin the other troops.

Nicholas strode to the front of the wagon and took his place at one of the long handles used to pull it over the rocky terrain. From time to time, the others put their shoulders to the rear of the wagon to help the wheels over especially difficult ruts or up an incline.

"It could be worse," Owen said. "It's not the cliffs of Dover."

Benjamin huffed. "Or my Cornwall coastline."

The others took sides in a goodhearted debate around regional pride, while Nicholas paused briefly to wipe the sweat from his forehead. "I never thought I'd say it, but in times like this I miss the fog and rain of home."

Percy groaned. "I don't need another story about your family's castle in Cumbria..."

Nicholas laughed along with the others. Perhaps he had shared too much over time, but nine years away from home and eight of them in the Royal Navy with several of these men had led to many a repeated tale.

John switched places with Miles on the closest handle. "Never mind them. I like hearing your stories of home. Seems like a great place to live."

Nicholas nodded his appreciation, then encouraged the entire crew up the final rise toward the road where they would have easier terrain to navigate.

After a minute's rest to catch their breath and adjust their grip, he motioned them back into position. "Come along, men. The sooner we take the coast, the sooner we advance the front and can end this war and return home."

They weren't defending their homeland, but they still had something worth fighting for and he could see the resolve and determination on their faces.

As they continued down the road toward Popham's camp, his mind wandered.

What would home be like after all this time?

He knew the castle was likely the same but wondered about the gardens or how the trees had grown. Were there new buildings in Ravenglass? New families?

Of course, he had also changed over the years due to the things he'd seen that haunted his dreams. Perhaps that was why he so desperately clung to the memories of home.

And yet thoughts of home always led to Susannah.

What was she doing now? Did she still visit their waterfall? She would be nineteen now and fending off the suitors. Did she resent their betrothal? Had she received any of his rare letters home? In the years since hearing of her father's death, he had only received updates passed along by his father.

A mile down the road, they finally approached the outskirts of the infantry camp and angled toward where their tents were pitched beside the cannons.

Unfortunately, along the way they had to pass the hospital tent. And the row of bodies of those who had perished from disease or injuries being prepared for burial.

The bodies of men who somewhere had family who would mourn their loss.

"Sighing and moaning, on ilka green loaning. The flowers of the forest are all wede away."

Nicholas shook off the haunting melody and the reminder of his mortality. He could only pray that God would protect him and his men.

~January 1813

Susannah eyed the profusion of color inside Madame de Barbot's shop as the proprietress displayed swatches of fabric to pair with her sketches.

It would be a long morning, for in addition to updating Susan's wardrobe and commissioning a few pieces for her trousseau should an offer be forthcoming, Pru's debut required a complete outfitting.

Today's order would cost a tidy sum, but it could have been worse.

Frugality in the area of household management led to excess in their clothing budgets. However, since the season was already underway and the local elites garbed months ago, Lady Stanley believed the shop's lightened load lent itself to bargaining for a discount. Not to mention, fabrics previously rejected by other ladies could be acquired for half their original cost.

Yes, their budget was stretched further than it might have been, but Susannah would have preferred to frequent the establishment of a dressmaker who truly needed the business to survive.

But only a de Barbot gown would do for Lady Stanley and her daughters.

Susannah sighed and settled onto a corner chair. From past experience, she knew that fitting days could drag on and on while waiting her turn.

Usually she was content altering Susan's castoffs from last season or using interchangeable sashes with a single white gown to give the illusion of variety.

Except today she was to be fitted for a new gown for Pru's debut ball and already had her eye on a burgundy fabric that Susan had rejected as too dark. It would bring out the reddish tones in her own hair and set her apart for one night from the ordinary brown locks of her stepsisters.

After all, for Pru's debut, Susannah had to appear fashionable enough to blend in as one of the Stanley girls. Lady Stanley was happy to claim three daughters when it was likely to earn her favor in certain circles.

The rest of the time, Susannah was Anna, the invisible wallflower of a daughter who felt like a financial burden on the household despite carrying out many of the duties daily and being the only blood relative of the man whose fortune was being squandered.

If her father were able to know from the hereafter, she hoped he knew how hard she tried to get along for his sake. Even as she lost herself in the process.

Across the room, Susan's giggle drew her attention to their conversation about potential suitors.

It seemed Susan was hoping for a minor noble with a rich estate. Or else a dashing officer like her friend had landed despite not being as pretty or well-connected as herself. Meanwhile, Lady Stanley was quick to point out that a wealthy merchant or businessman would serve equally well in terms of a secure future.

Pru ignored them both, reaching instead for a biscuit from the tea tray the proprietress had supplied. Until her mother stopped her with a quick slap of her folded fan.

Susannah felt a bit sorry for the girl who had been put on a strict diet but now, while still plump, she fit the image expected for debutantes.

The gossip shifted toward speculation on who might or might not be in attendance at various upcoming events and Susannah's mind wandered back to last year's excruciating joint debut with Susan since they were close in age.

All preferential attention was paid to the eldest, but Susannah was more than happy to fade into the background. Especially since she was not in the market for a husband.

In the months since, she had already discouraged several suitors and deflected them in Susan's direction.

Why was she still hiding the fact she was already betrothed?

Did she fear reprisal due to jealousy? Or worry that such a dream was too good to be true and he would pick another bride?

Although both were partially true, mostly she kept her secrets because her memories of Nicholas were a precious treasure from her past that she would never allow the others to sully if she could prevent it.

But none of it mattered unless she heard from Muncaster.

Susannah picked at a loose thread on her skirt.

During a shopping trip to the local market at the beginning of her debut season, she had personally posted another letter to Sir Thomas at Muncaster informing him that if he heard the rumors of her debut, she was simply biding her time until Nicholas' return and notifying him that her address was still the same.

She had not received anything from Ravenglass in years but suspected her stepmother of interference again.

Perhaps she should confide in the woman enough to gain her permission for correspondence, but truly feared her reaction.

Who else did she have to hold her confidences?

Lucy's loyalties lay with her employer and Susannah had few friends. One might suggest the local clergy as a source of advice, but she already knew that Bishop Langley's attention was captured by money and position...of which they had little. Despite her father's title, the Stanleys were among the faceless relatively poor masses unworthy of his time.

Minutes turned into hours, but just as Susannah's stomach was about to growl from hunger, the conversation finally turned to her wardrobe selections and she made her way over to the modiste's station.

Lady Stanley must have been fatigued from her previous decisions for she offered little protest when Susannah made her fabric selection from among Susan's rejects.

However, while updating Susannah's measurements, the proprietress caught sight of the still visible scar on her arm. "Perhaps a style with long sleeves to conceal your flaw? Or gloves since they are still in style."

"She already has gloves that will suffice." Lady Stanley glared at the fact Susannah had revealed her defect in the presence of a stranger.

Madame de Barbot frowned. "I see. However, with shorter sleeves, you will need a cloak. I can add a fur lining in the hood for additional warmth—"

"And an additional expense." Lady Stanley sniffed. "She will survive without the fur."

Susannah kept her expression calm lest she risk losing the new cloak as well.

She wished she could sew her fur into the hood herself later just like she had in the past. However, even if the remaining pieces were in good enough condition, her stepmother was sure to notice the extravagance.

Instead, the scraps would have to remain in the box in the base of her wardrobe on the third floor along with her other treasures worth protecting.

Over the course of her nineteen years, she had lost her parents, her brother, her home, and even her real name. It was little wonder that she clung to the memories wherever she could.

Madame de Barbot sighed as if a fur-free cloak were a travesty, but moved on to review the list of garments. After finalizing their order, she stood and walked them toward the door. "I thank you for your repeated business. You will soon be costumed well enough to travel in circles with the Regent himself."

From her position at the rear of the party, Susannah grimaced. From what she had heard of the pompous prince, he was not that much of an improvement over their aging monarch. But such was the reality of inherited positions versus those who merited them.

"...However, even if you never venture to London, now that Wellington is finally pushing Napoleon's troops out of Spain for good, soon all those dashing British war heroes and officers will be back on the marriage market." The modiste winked at Susan in particular.

Susan and Pru giggled while her stepmother's lips curved in a smug smile.

Those rumors were true...along with reports of the mounting numbers of dead.

Please God, let Nicholas be among the returned...

Because if she didn't have that future to look forward to, she had nothing left.

Chapter Five

S o many were dead, and yet the battle to retake Maya Pass continued.

After his crew reloaded their cannon on the western ridge, Nicholas took aim at an outcropping of rock shielding two score of French firing down upon the advancing British troops.

Wellington's forces had laid siege to the port of San Sebastian and town of Pamplona, forcing Napoleon's armies to abandon their last strongholds in Spain.

However, it seemed the French were now mounting an offensive through the Pyrenees mountains to provide reinforcements to those stranded garrisons.

His crew had been assigned to help guard Maya Pass, however the commander of the 2nd Division did not fully comprehend the looming threat posed by the handful of French soldiers spotted earlier in the day. The full force attack came suddenly and the British forces in the valley had finally reached the top of the pass only to discover it was now overrun with thousands of French soldiers seeking an avenue into the heart of Spain.

Though vastly outnumbered, the British troops were currently fighting against the odds to retake the pass or at least hold back the French in the narrow canyon...

"Stand by." He called the warning, touched the match to the firing tube, then covered his ears. With the explosion still ringing in his ears, his crew hurried to swab out the barrel, load the fixed round, and ram it home. Meanwhile, he studied the impact of the previous shell already calculating the trajectory of the next shot before they moved on to a new target.

It did not matter that he was a knight or an officer in Navy blue, he still had to deal with the suction of muck on his boots after the rain and the vermin-ridden meal stores at camp.

And now he was stuck in this mountainous hellhole away from the sea.

Just a few days ago, he'd compared the current terrain of the Pyrenees to that of his beloved Cumbria. But today the screams of the wounded pierced the air as frequently as the musket fire that left gray wisps of smoke wafting over the valley had erased all sense of beauty, leaving behind blood-soaked earth.

It was a majestic land reduced by violent conflict.

He fired the cannon again, but it did little to deter the enemy's advance and too many lives had already been lost.

A shout from behind relayed the order for them to withdraw from the crest and pull back to a new position.

He nodded his acknowledgment, then began to calculate their egress route. But a speedy glance over his shoulder revealed that the main force of British soldiers was already in full retreat with none staying to provide cover for his crew to remove their gun, especially over this steep terrain.

His heart leapt in his chest.

His crew was fully exposed on the crest and it would take time to move their gun. Time they did not have as the French were already advancing.

He would have to make the impossible choice to abandon or destroy the gun as they ran for safety. Or help guard the retreat and risk capture or worse since they had one rifle among them.

Only one path rang true in his heart but would his men obey his orders?

Benjamin was the first to speak as he rammed another round into place. "There is no way to save the cannon, but we can still protect the wounded."

"Aye." The others agreed with grim expressions, although he did not miss John's longing glance toward the valley and the dwindling number of red coated infantry.

"So be it." Nicholas waited as Owen pierced the cloth powder bag through the cannon's vent hole and inserted the priming tube. "Let's make our last shots matter before we tumble her into the ravine."

He calculated a new angle to hinder the French advancement on the eastern flank of limping wounded straggling behind and barked directions to John and Percy to adjust the elevation. Once they were in position, he lifted the smoldering match.

"Stand by." He touched the firing tube and turned away from the blast, already choosing the next target. Except in so doing, he spotted a small group of enemy soldiers circling around to ambush their position.

If they were going to disable the cannon as well, they would only have one shot left. *God, help me to save the lives of my countrymen.*

Out of the corner of his eye, he saw a French officer on horseback surrounded by several men with semaphore flags. Disrupting the chain of command and communication even for a minute would aid the escape.

As the crew reloaded, he moved the cannon into the new position. "Miles, fire the last shot when ready, then Benjamin, let's shove her over the edge." He could only hope the hot metal of the barrel would bend and dent upon impact on the rocks below and be rendered useless.

He reached for their rifle and prepared to target the lead soldier of the ambushing party. Except once their element of surprise was lost, the French ducked into hiding...effectively cutting off his crew's path of escape in the process.

Beyond them, the last of the British troops were approaching the bend in the valley. At least their sacrifice had saved many lives

"Stand by."

A moment later, the explosion echoed in the valley, followed by the low grunts of his loyal crew.

Now someone had to save their lives in return...

As much as it galled him, at the crashing sound of the tumbling cannon, he tied his handkerchief on the rifle barrel and raised it in surrender.

Dear Lord, let the enemy have mercy.

A blur of activity and shouts to his left were followed by a blinding pain in the side of his head.

Pain stabbed his head as the cannon crashed into the ravine beside a waterfall. A girl's voice sang of flowers, and then she screamed as she too fell over the edge.

"Susannah!"

Nicholas awakened with a jolt and a nauseating pain that originated on the left side of his head above his eye. He moaned at the reminder that he was in a dark barn along with other captured soldiers.

As the light grew gradually brighter through the cracks in the walls, he had a vague sense of the passage of time. He did not think this was his first morning in the makeshift prison, but perhaps his second.

He slowly raised a hand to the blood-stiffened bandage on his aching head as the memories returned.

Despite his signal of surrender, he had been clubbed with a rifle stock. And in addition to the agonizing and blinding headache, he grew dizzy whenever he moved fast. Others in his crew had been equally roughed up before being marched north to join other prisoners who had already been held long enough for infection to set in. Disease and malnutrition would be next.

At least his crew were all there. For now.

However, if they did not figure out how to escape soon, they would perish. Especially if the French pushed back into Spain.

With the dawn of another day, more of the others awoke.

A stranger nearby was the first to speak. "You were talking in your sleep. Who is Susannah?"

He held his breath. What had he said in his dreams?

Owen's voice cut through the dim interior. "We don't have anywhere else to go so you might as well tell them all of your stories. Anything to get our tortured minds off the stench of this place."

If it would help pass the time, he was willing. Just not to share the precious details of his Susannah and their one and only true meeting.

Nicholas carefully pushed up onto one elbow and leaned against the rough boards of the wall. "Susannah is my betrothed but it has been years since I last saw her. Her father was a knight of the realm near the village of Boot in the Eskdale valley in the Lake District in the far north of England. Cumbria." He sighed. "With the most beautiful fells and falls you ever did see. This Pyrenees area reminds me of those valleys, but the Esk is where I first met Susannah while rambling the countryside."

He smiled at the memories and could almost smell the damp foliage around their waterfall.

"Tell them about your castle, Sir Nicholas." Benjamin's voice held a touch of laughter.

A few of the other prisoners murmured that he could not really have a title...until Percy and Miles pantomimed his knighting ceremony, complete with a fake sword tapped on the other's shoulders and an exaggerated but deferential *my liege*.

Nicholas joined their laughter and embraced the change in topic. "My father is a baronet—Sir Thomas Pennington—and therefore as his heir, I have been a knight for the past four years. Some of these men were at the ceremony with our captain, although their depiction is not quite how I remembered it."

Several of his crew members laughed and it lifted his spirits. But in order to distract the rest of the prisoners, he continued his story.

"Muncaster Castle has been in our family for over 600 years. It is nearest to Ravenglass on the west Cumbrian coast just over one hundred miles north of Liverpool and sixty miles south of Scotland."

"Enough geography, how big is the castle?"

"Do you have jewels there?"

"Did anything or anyone famous happen or stay there?"

The story of a castle had enlivened many and he caught John's grin and Owen's nod. And somehow his head did not pain him as much when Benjamin helped him to a full sitting position.

"Anyone famous? Would King Henry the Sixth be famous enough?" Nicholas paused for effect before continuing. "According to tradition, after the Battle of Towton during the Wars of the Roses, King Henry fled to Muncaster and found shelter with my ancestor John Pennington. When he departed, he left behind a glass drinking bowl in hopes that my family would prosper as long as it remained unbroken." He grinned. "Almost 400 years later, it is still intact and we call it the Luck of Muncaster."

"Luck? Then how did you come to end up here?"

The brash question and the sound of keys on the lock outside deflated their elevated morale.

A moment later, their captors opened the door. This time he was alert enough to notice the sagging hinges and see more of the rustic barn where they were confined. Despite wincing at the bright light of the rising sun shining in through the doorway, he caught glimpses of the enemy encampment beyond the armed guards who left a bucket of water near the door and tossed a few hard rolls to the dirt before exiting and locking the door once again.

They had stayed less than a minute and not ventured beyond a foot of the entrance. Would they have even noticed if the number of prisoners had diminished?

Even in their weakened state, it would not take much effort for the prisoners to loosen a hinge and tip the door to create a gap big enough to squeeze through.

He listened carefully for another minute to confirm, but it seemed the noise from the encampment only came from that side of their makeshift prison. Meaning they must be on the outskirts of camp with perhaps only a sentry to deal with on the perimeter.

Nicholas was still lost in thought when John handed him some of the bread. "What are you thinking?"

Nicholas glanced around, then lowered his voice. "I know I was mostly incoherent yesterday, but what have you noticed about our guards?" In the dim light, he scanned the rest of the building for structural weaknesses especially away from the main door.

"What do you mean?"

"How often do they come with food or water? Do they only linger by the door or venture further? And do the guards ever check for injuries or the dead or even count the prisoners?"

John's answers confirmed his earlier observations, but his voice carried and a few others took interest in their conversation.

About the time Owen gathered the rest of the Superb's crew into their corner, Nicholas spotted another door with even worse hinges than the main door. He had to assume it was barred or locked from the outside as well, but it was located on the side furthest from the camp and surrounded by rotting wood. Any tampering they did would be less noticeable and based on the direction of the rising sun, traveling west would naturally take them closer to Wellington's troops and even the coast with access to naval ships.

He bit into the stale roll and chewed slowly as his ideas took shape.

"What do you need us to do?" Benjamin handed him a tin cup of water.

Nicholas nodded his thanks and took a long drink, letting his body absorb the sustenance. It galled him to be so physically weak as to require their help, but even in his current state, he could be strong enough to give them hope and an escape.

And by the time they were prepared to run, he prayed his injury would be less of a hindrance.

He handed the cup back, then leaned against the wall. "We will need to work together, but I believe we can all escape under cover of night."

That declaration caught everyone's attention and soon they had devised a plan to create an opening in the back of the barn during the day when any noise they made was muffled by the general activity of the encampment. Others would continually observe through the cracks in the walls to scout their surroundings and establish a pattern for the camp sentries. Then under cover of darkness, they could slip out into the woods and head west.

"If my vague memory of how far we were marched is correct, in about six miles or so, we should run into the River Bidassoa and cross into Spain where we're likely to run into our troops and—"

He gestured to his officer's coat and a few others with military issued uniform pieces. "—assure them of our identities."

He looked into the eyes of the other prisoners one by one.

Men who were now depending on him for their freedom.

"We are going to get out of this hell hole."

* * *

The following night, Nicholas pushed on the bottom corner of the dilapidated door until it pivoted on the upper hinge, then peeked out the resulting gap.

He was the last to exit their prison and knew John was likely still crouched next to building waiting to dart across the fifteen feet of open space to reach the trees. In making their plans, they had decided to stagger their runs to minimize noise and avoid detection but it had slowed their departure.

In the faint light of the moon, he spotted Benjamin's bulk under a tree where he directed the others—mostly infantry including several who were very sick and therefore supported by fellow soldiers—to the west where Owen was to lead the way.

He did not feel that strong himself, but the adrenaline of his impending escape was helping him to forget the dull pounding inside his skull.

Ahead, he saw the shadowed ridge and hoped the first prisoners to leave were already beyond it and out of sight.

With the coast clear, he squeezed his body through the opening, then reached back to replace the door and erase the scuff marks in the dirt beneath his boots. Their escape would be clearly noticed in the morning, but the longer it took to discover their route, the higher their chances of being rescued before being recaptured.

A stick snapped in the woods and he held his breath. Had a misstep in the dark doomed them all?

Benjamin stared back with wide eyes.

To Nicholas' right, a voice called out in French and soon he heard the footsteps of an approaching sentry.

They were out of time.

Nicholas waved Benjamin out of sight, took a deep breath, then ran toward the trees headed to the south. Perhaps he could still escape, but at least his pounding feet and the noise of breaking branches tugging at his clothes might deflect attention away from the bulk of the escapees. And the barn.

Almost immediately he heard footsteps at his back and then John's huffing voice. "Now we are creating a diversion?"

"I am sorry." He had not meant to bring the other man to probable doom and yet he was glad not to be alone.

At first, he sought only to put distance between himself and the enemy without concern for the amount of noise that would signal an obvious place to send a larger search party.

Someone shouted back at the camp.

The escape had been discovered.

Nicholas pushed on through the trees with John right beside him.

A rifle fired and almost immediately he felt a stinging heat in his left shoulder. He gasped, then clutched the injury with warm liquid dripping between his fingers.

John wrapped an arm around his waist to support him, then detoured them quietly off their original route and to the west..

Please God, let the others get to safety. And hide us from the enemy.

Once they were over a small rise, John whispered in his ear. "Just a bit more. I see a spot to rest."

Nicholas concentrated on keeping his feet moving and desire to moan contained as John changed their course once again and pulled them into a shadowed space beneath an outcropping of rock.

Huddled together in the dark, Nicholas fought to catch his breath but it was difficult since he was already dizzy from exertion after the head injury and now from blood loss. He could not keep going without bandaging the wound.

He clenched his teeth to prevent a sound, then John helped him remove his officer's coat. He glanced at his blood-soaked shirt and poked with his fingers.

It appeared the bullet had gone straight through but he would need bandaging.

He removed his shirt and then with a whisper, instructed John to tear the fabric into strips. It took longer than expected while avoiding making excess noise, but before long his wound had been packed, wrapped, and more strips of fabric used to tie his arm across his chest for support.

The situation reminded him of when it was Susannah wearing his shirt as bandages.

Would he survive to see her again?

Once bandaged, Nicholas leaned back against the rock and tried to rest while he could. Fortunately, it seemed the bleeding had slowed.

He and John both listened to the forest sounds. There had been a few distant shouts, but none drew closer to their current position. And to his great relief, it seemed they had truly diverted the search away from the rest of the prisoners.

Hopefully he would see them again soon.

In the meantime, he and John were safe in the darkness. But daylight would provide new challenges.

As he rested to regain his strength, Nicholas tried to recall the geography.

To the south was the pass and their previous battleground. But further south was also Spain with various British military divisions scattered along the border.

Their best hope was to angle south and west to reach the river, their allies, or eventually the coast. But they would need to travel at night and rest during the day until they were sure they had evaded the searchers.

And they could not afford to waste the waning hours before dawn.

He leaned close to John and whispered the plan. "You may have to help me, but we need more distance and a better hiding place for when the day breaks."

John eyed Nicholas' injuries as if in doubt of his survival, but eventually nodded.

Bracing himself for the pain, Nicholas started to put his coat back on but John stopped him.

"Your arm won't fit in the sleeve and the dangling fabric might only snag on branches and leave a trail. I can wear it for now..."

He could have tucked the sleeve inside and the warmth would have been welcome, but too weary to argue, he passed the coat to John and staggered to his feet.

After erasing any evidence of their short stay, including blood drops, Nicholas gritted his teeth against the pain and followed John into the dark woods.

Days later, Nicholas sat propped against a tree to rest as the sun began to rise. He inhaled deep breaths of the salt-tinged air from the ocean nearby but his head still whirled from another night spent walking.

After a long trek through the mountains in the dark while avoiding roads, they had come upon a farm and hidden in a loaded wagon in order to avoid a patrol.

Only to awaken to movement as the wagon's owner drove much further south into Spain bypassing the English troop encampments completely. After much debate, instead of retracing their path north hoping to stumble upon Wellington's land army, he and John made for the coastline.

They were finally back near the ocean and hoped to spot a friendly ship to signal. Or recruit a kindly villager to relay a message to the army.

The worst that could happen was they would have to retrace their journey back toward enemy territory to rejoin their unit.

However, Nicholas himself was their biggest problem.

He was feverish from the festering shoulder wound, parched, famished, and stumbling on his feet.

Which was why John had left him here and ventured alone into the village just over the rise to round up provisions.

John.

Nicholas frowned.

There was something odd about the man. And not just his obvious frustrations that Nicholas' health was hindering their pace and putting him at risk of discovery.

No. It was the topics of their conversations while resting during the day.

John refused to talk of his home or family, but endlessly peppered Nicholas for descriptions of Ravenglass, the people, and Muncaster Castle. Nicholas purposely ignored the few invasive questions about his betrothed, but Susannah was not far from his mind.

The man had said the questions were to keep Nicholas' spirits up by focusing on the future since a hopeful outlook was necessary for the body to heal. But then John hinted that since he had nothing left to go home to, he himself might like to find a position or role in business in the north.

Of course, Nicholas offered his assistance in appreciation for the man's help over the last few days and for not leaving him behind.

But now that he was alone, doubts resurfaced and nagged like the ants crawling across his exposed skin.

Why the secrecy? And why the sudden interest in Nicholas' life?

Not to mention the man continued to find excuses to wear Nicholas' coat. He claimed it was because the wounds needed air between their re-bandaging attempts, but the last time Nicholas asked for the warmth to fight off the feverish chills, the possessive gleam in John's eyes put him on edge.

And today he'd insisted it was needed as an obviously British symbol to recruit local allies and assistance.

If only Nicholas wasn't so weak, he would demand his property back and wear it himself into the village.

A series of shouts came from over the rise.

Nicholas sat up tall, then felt the urgency to get his feet underneath him.

To slip further into the trees.

John appeared at the top of the slope, running with empty arms and motioning for Nicholas to get moving.

They must have been discovered.

Nicholas turned and staggered as fast as he was able back into the cover. He sucked in breaths against the pain and held his flaming shoulder with his free hand.

But why would John lead the enemy toward Nicholas' hiding place?

Why not divert attention away like Nicholas had done back at the barn?

Behind him came a shout in an unfamiliar language.

Not French. Not Spanish or Portuguese either.

He risked a glance backward and saw John almost upon him and not far behind...

A glimpse of skin colors and clothing that sent icy dread to his heart.

Pirates.

Despite the British rule of the seas, the brigands from the Barbary coast continued to raid and pillage Spanish villages taking not only foodstuffs and gold, but also capturing people. While they would ransom the titled or wealthy, most were enslaved and sold into Africa.

Fear lent a burst of speed to his feet as Nicholas focused on his escape.

Dear God, save us.

John darted past him, leading the way into the underbrush but no longer helping Nicholas. As if he was only willing to save himself now.

Anger flared at the cowardice of his fellow sailor. A man he had once handpicked to be a part of his shore-bound gunnery crew.

A sudden blow from behind sent Nicholas careening into a tree, simultaneously impacting his already-injured head and shoulder. With the cracking sound of breaking ribs and a flash of pain, he ricocheted off the obstacle and landed heavily on the rocky ground.

He gasped for breath and clung to consciousness as the pirates rushed past him, still in pursuit.

In the distance, he heard a struggle and John saying something about a ransom.

Nearer by, with darkness encroaching on his vision and blood trickling down his face, he spied a cluster of small blue flowers.

The flowers of the forest are all withered away.

Chapter Six

~September 7, 1813

It had been five years since her last birthday celebration, and once again there would be no cake unless she baked it herself. No one to wish her well or acknowledge that she had reached her twentieth year.

Only yards of woodwork to polish in the entryway before the dinner party she was to prepare and serve...but not attend.

She rubbed her cloth along the paneling with more force than normal.

Every day it became more difficult than ever to hold onto hope. But according to the rumors at the market yesterday, Wellington's forces were pushing further north into France and the end of the war was in sight even if it took another year.

If Nicholas was unable to return for her before that year passed, once she was twenty-one, she would apply for a governess or domestic servant position elsewhere just to get away from the Stanley household before resentment and bitterness ate away at the shredded remnants of her soul.

Tears stung her eyes.

One would think she would be accustomed to the years of neglect and being brushed aside. However, last week she had overheard her stepmother talking to Susan and Pru about their marital prospects including a handsome young merchant who had caught Susan's eye.

Life might be simpler once one or both of the girls were married.

Yet in the course of the conversation, she learned that offers for her own hand had been summarily declined. In fact, Pru had laughed at Susan's observation that her red hair perfectly matched her work-calloused hands.

Meanwhile her stepmother's assessment hurt the worst. *What do they see in her? She's nothing but a scarred backwoods orphan who doesn't have an inkling of how to interact in proper society.*

Not that she had been given a chance once her mourning period had expired.

Susannah took a deep breath and scrubbed all the harder.

Proper society? Once upon a time she had visited Muncaster Castle and stood beside the Duke of Middlesbrough who complimented her singing. She would almost think she had imagined the whole celebration, if not for the existence of a new gown sewn by the dressmaker from Carlile.

A brisk knock interrupted her musings and knowing Duncan was fetching a delivery of wood, she opened the front door and received a letter by special delivery.

A letter addressed to Miss Susannah Stanley.

Sent from Muncaster.

It was the best of gifts.

A smile stretched her face and she clutched the missive to her chest for a few precious moments before sinking to the bottom stair and breaking the elaborate seal.

Susannah,

Forgive my lapse in regular correspondence but at last there is news from the continent. My son has been captured by pirates and since he is both a noble and an officer, he is being held for ransom.

She gasped, then pressed a hand to her mouth as she read on.

However, there is a mediator in place to serve as my representative. I have already authorized the payment and am on my way to London to await his arrival.

At least there was hope of redemption. *Dear God, keep Nicholas safe and bring him safely home.*

I cannot express how I long to see my dear Nicholas again. Every day that passes is filled with regret over sending him to sea, but I cannot contain my pride at the man he has become. I pray he has not been too changed by his experiences, but I have no doubt he is a true credit to the Pennington name.

My dear, in addition to making you aware of his impending return, I wish for you to begin preparations for the wedding. I cannot wait to have family here in the castle again...and if I may be so bold, I look forward to the next generation of Penningtons and the pitter patter of little feet in the hallways of Muncaster.

After all these years, you are fully grown and I wonder if I will even recognize you. Certainly, such a reunion will be even more a shock for Nicholas...

She had thought receiving a letter was a gift, but her heart nearly burst with joy to know she would soon have a reason to leave Liverpool behind and create a family of her own.

Her eyes pored over the letter a second time, treasuring each and every word.

"What is the meaning of this idleness?"

Susannah jumped to her feet as her stepmother descended the stairs but could not hide the parchment in time.

"And reading mail that doesn't belong to you? For shame, Anna."

"It is mine."

Lady Stanley snatched the letter from her hand, then glanced at the front. "This is addressed to Susan—"

"Nay. To Susannah. To me." She lifted her chin and for once stood her ground as receiving the letter had restored her hope for the future. "And for what purpose would Sir Thomas write to Susan at all? Since he was often away on business, I doubt he'd ever met her in the short time you lived in Boot."

"Silence!" Her stepmother turned away in order to read the letter.

Her chest burned with anger to see those precious words violated by her stepmother's eyes but she had little chance of retrieving the missive without damaging the parchment.

The woman spun back to face her with a mottled face. "What is this about a wedding? Who is getting married?"

Susannah swallowed hard. "I am." The moment to reveal the truth had come at the worst possible moment as her stepsisters were already descending the stairs, drawn by their mother's shrill voice.

She braced her shoulders and met their eyes before looking back to her stepmother. "I have been betrothed for the past seven years. Since before Father married you."

"He never said anything—"

"Why should he? Decisions about his daughter's future had nothing to do with you and there was plenty of time to share the details later." Somewhere within her slight frame, the daughter her parents had raised was breaking free.

Her father's second wife sneered. "But you have had ample time to tell me. Why waste my money on gowns for a debut you never needed? Are you a thief as well as a liar?"

Susannah chose to ignore the inflammatory judgments on her character. "Nicholas has been at war for almost a decade and many of our men have not returned. With no guarantee of a wedding, what harm was there in keeping an open mind? Not to mention, you demanded I be there for Susan and Pru's debuts as part of the family. Even if I am a scarred backwoods orphan, I had to dress the part."

She bit her lip to stop the verbal flood as all of the emotions bottled up since her father's death threatened to come pouring out. The release might feel good but would only make things worse.

A shrewd gleam lit her stepmother's eyes. "Was there a written betrothal contract or merely a verbal agreement of understanding? After all, you are not of age and I can block any wedding if I so choose."

Her breath caught with the sudden fear that her private papers might be destroyed out of spite if their existence were revealed. She blinked several times before answering. "I was not acquainted with Father's files, however..." She took advantage of their proximity and her stepmother's distraction to retrieve her letter. "It appears Sir Thomas Pennington has no doubts. Perhaps you should take up the matter with him when he returns from London with his son."

"Pennington? As in Muncaster Castle?" Pru's question echoed off the half-polished woodwork.

"What would they want with the likes of her?" Susan's scorn felt like a blow. "Then again, if she is telling the truth, it is no wonder she has always thought herself better than us."

Tears once again threatened at the injustice.

She tucked the letter away in the pocket of her apron so as not to lose it again and gathered her cleaning supplies. "If you'll excuse me, I have much still to do today." She walked away but not without the heat of glares at her back.

As she had feared, the announcement of her betrothal had revealed the depths of their jealous hatred. And given her a glimpse of her stepmother's plans to block the marriage.

She could only hope that Nicholas was willing to fight yet another battle for her hand.

In the meantime, it was going to be a long few months waiting for her hero to set foot on English soil again.

Nicholas awoke in the sweltering overcrowded bagnio and blinked several times. The lingering lilt of a song and the mist of a crashing waterfall were fading fast.

Another dream.

While the current mixture of pain and filth and stench was all too real.

Barring a miracle, this was his future as a slave in a Moroccan port.

Home was but a distant memory.

He clutched his side as he sat up from his position on the woven mat that provided the only reprieve from the stone floor each night.

The sharp pain in his ribs that had plagued him for weeks after his capture was now only a dull ache if he moved too suddenly. His headaches had ceased, the mental fog had lifted, and the festering wound in his shoulder had also finally healed.

Nicholas stretched the sore muscles in his arms and back from working long hours every day.

The bullet wound had been helped along after being doused in salt water as he, John, and the other captives from the village they'd been near were dragged through the surf to the pirates' ship.

While there were unbelievably cramped quarters in the belly of the ship where additional captives from previous raids were already kept, the reprieve from running across the countryside had allowed his body to begin to heal.

Nicholas turned to rouse the ailing man nearby. "Are you coming, my friend?"

"Si, mi amigo." Stefan groaned, then stood. "Right behind you."

Nicholas staggered toward the basket of bread and the buckets of fresh water to drink. He gnawed the food like an animal despite knowing it would do little to ease the knot of hunger twisting his midsection.

It wasn't much for a breakfast but he'd seen the punishment for those who complained. And for those who were late to report to their work assignments.

Having his feet beaten until he could not walk would not improve his chances of ever finding a way to escape.

The community's slave quarters were clearing out for the day as the occupants ventured out as servants and laborers.

With Stefan behind him, he stepped out into the open air, past two turbaned guards with vicious scimitars, and turned toward the docks. At least he had made a friend here, for he would hate to be alone in these circumstances.

After years fighting in Spain, Nicholas had picked up enough of the language to communicate somewhat. But to meet a man of Spanish heritage captured from an American vessel had been a surprise. Although he was glad the man spoke decent English most of the time.

Nicholas had patiently listened while the man had grieved the loss of his family since only the men were taken captive while the women and children were slaughtered and tossed overboard. Stefan's shock had given way to anger and eventually a bitter acceptance. Only Nicholas' prodding had kept the man moving forward and eating enough to stay alive although a loose cough now kept the man up for hours at night and he was still short of breath during the day.

They continued on past the ornate building where immediately upon arrival six weeks ago they were paraded before the local ruler.

With a wave of the man's bejeweled hand, John was taken away with other healthy captives while Nicholas was ridiculed for his claim of a title before being escorted out with the injured and weak only to be put in a dank cellar overnight before taken to the market.

It still vexed him to have been stripped, examined, prodded, and humiliatingly sold...but at least someone saw his potential when healed and now he labored near the ocean, loading and unloading ship's cargo in a warehouse.

But where had John ended up?

Anger flared.

They had been separated almost immediately once aboard the pirate ship. However, even if his fever had fueled his vague memories of a discussion about a ransom, since he had been wearing Nicholas' officer's coat, John had probably bargained for an easier job in a rich household instead of that of a common laborer.

However, as they passed by a string of galley slaves being herded toward a ship, he knew his own fate could have been worse. The rumor around the bagnio was that those poor souls were chained below decks on a ship and left to labor, sleep, and even defecate in one spot for months at a time.

Even in slavery, he had much to be thankful for.

He slowed his steps as they approached the final street, giving Stefan time to catch his breath enough to avoid a coughing fit. A minute later, the man nodded and they continued on to the warehouse where their bearded taskmaster already waited.

Using hand signals, Assad pointed out a stack of wooden crates to be moved from the rear of the warehouse and stacked on a wagon near the entrance.

They were always under the man's supervision. Lifting and carrying. Opening some crates and then closing others. Even replacing broken slats on a few.

It was mindless work for the slaves and other workers while the master profited from the buying and selling of goods. The type of transactions his own father would appreciate.

A wave of bitterness soured his mouth for it was that desire for his son to learn the merchant trade that set him on this path to begin with.

Was Nicholas still a credit to the Pennington name now? Would anyone even notify his father of his capture and recapture? Or would his sire give up hope believing him to be dead?

Oh, how easy it was to fall into despair. Or bitterness and regret. Or anger.

He shook his head to stop the thoughts.

There would be time enough for revenge on the pirates or even the French later. For now, he needed to be strong mentally as well as physically.

Nearby, Stefan slowed his steps to keep his breathing under control and the coughs at bay. Nicholas automatically stepped in front of his friend to shield him from Assad's view, then chose one of the heavier crates, whistling to attract attention as he hoisted it onto the wagon.

Anything to keep Assad from applying the whip to Stefan's back and delaying his recovery once again.

As they passed by each other on his return to the back of the warehouse, Stefan nodded to acknowledge the help then cracked a rare smile. "I thank you, Sir Nicholas."

A few minutes later, Nicholas took advantage of his height to lift Stefan's crate onto the top of the stack.

The man smiled again. "Is that your idea of a castle?"

He grinned, then held his fingers inches apart. "A small one. How do you say...pequeño?" Like his shipmates before him, Stefan had endured more than a few stories of Nicholas' former life.

A pile of crates was nothing like Muncaster, and yet his memories of home gave him the incentive to plan an escape and return someday.

If he did, what would he find there?

Like in his dreams, his mind resurrected thoughts of his sweet Susannah with a crown of flowers in her hair. Then wounded lying among the rhododendrons...and yet brave and trusting. Calling him her hero.

The conjured images of greenery and flowers from the Eskdale valley almost had him imagining the sea breeze from home and not the stagnant spicy smells of a Moroccan port.

After transferring a few more crates, the loaded wagon rolled out toward the quay and Assad pointed to a broom. Their order to clean up.

While Stefan swept the stone floor of bits of debris, Nicholas arranged emptied crates on the shelves in an orderly fashion, then stacked the extra boards they used for repairs.

Moving through the repetitive task allowed his mind to wander once again toward home.

What if he were to create a flat space to the east of the castle overlooking the valley and line that terrace with trimmed hedges? He could then have a garden space in which to recreate the valley's beauty closer to the castle grounds and even transplant several varieties of greenery along with flowers...

A smile curved his lips.

He might be held hostage by the Barbary pirates, but he could still find his way home if only in his mind.

Susannah once said she believed he could do anything he set his mind to. He might be a captive but he was still free to dream and imagine beauty...

Chapter Seven

~*Late September*

Susannah and their housemaid Lucy were in the midst of scrubbing the last of the linens with lye soap when Pru intruded and wrinkled her nose.

"Anna, Mother said for you to come to the drawing room for a family meeting."

Susannah sighed. "Tell her that I will be along shortly once these are rinsed and hung to dry."

"Leave it to the maid." Pru turned on her heel and left in a swirl of skirts.

"You had better go, miss." Lucy blew a strand of hair from her eyes. "I can see to the rest."

Susannah rinsed the caustic residue from her skin, then dried her hands on her apron. "They are most likely planning another dinner party and wish to arrange the menu, but I'll return as soon as I'm able."

However, upon entering the drawing room and seeing the twisted smile on her stepmother's face, she braced herself for their latest source of entertainment—dreaming up punishments for trivial perceived infractions.

The woman waved her to a seat opposite where her daughters were paired on a couch. "I have received some news that might interest you."

Susannah perched on the edge of the chair and inclined her head.

Her stepmother lifted a letter from her lap and began to read. "Dear Miss Stanley, I regret—"

"What? Is that addressed to me?" She rose to her feet. "Why ever did you intercept private correspondence?" Dread pooled in her midsection for only a few would have written to her at this address and one of them had recently addressed her more familiarly...

"Silence! This is my household and you will hold your impertinence." Lady Stanley's eyes flashed her rage. "I fear I granted you too much leeway in your time of loss but now it is time to repay my generosity."

Shock had Susannah collapsing back in her seat. "Generosity?" Since when did secondhand gowns and a long list of chores fit in that description?

"Of course. There was nothing in your father's will to say that I had to care for his daughter. The inheritance was for me alone to use at my discretion. And now it seems God has provided a means for you to pay your debt."

She was rendered speechless. Surely her father would never have left her without recourse but those days surrounding the funeral were a blur. And she'd been barely fifteen.

Susannah glanced at the sisters. Pru looked completely surprised but Susan's greedy smile mimicked that of her mother.

What debt did she owe Lady Stanley? And what means did she have to pay?

She rubbed her forehead in confusion.

Who had been the solicitor to deliver the news of the bequests? Or should she contact her distant cousin directly to inquire about temporary shelter so as to remove herself from this household? Wait. Wouldn't she be technically the ward of... Of who? That same relative or Sir Thomas? Why had she not thought of that sooner?

"Aren't you the least bit curious?" Her stepmother lifted the letter again and smirked.

Susannah swallowed hard. "I am sure you are eager to enlighten me." Not the humblest thing to say but how could her life get any worse?

"This is from a Mr. Ellis. Apparently he is the steward at Muncaster Castle."

She did not recognize the name but then again, it had been five years since the aged steward had extended condolences after her father's funeral.

Lady Stanley tapped the parchment. "Dear Miss Stanley, I regret to inform you of the tragic events of a week past. Sir Thomas had been in London to await the arrival of the envoy and a group of captives. Details are limited but sometime shortly after his reunion with Sir Nicholas, they were attacked by thieves while still on the dock. Both were injured and unfortunately Sir Thomas perished a short time later."

Her heart raced leaving her lightheaded.

Reunited only to be attacked, injured, and...dead? Poor Nicholas to have suffered so much already only to bear more pain and grief.

Her stepmother continued reading as if nothing were amiss. "The Pennington's London agent sent word that the body is being transported by sea back to Cumbria for burial while Sir Nicholas wishes to convalesce and mourn privately at home."

If only she could be there to comfort and support him the way he had lightened her burdens when she had been crying beside a waterfall.

A strand of woven flowers would do little to ease his sorrow, but she was already mentally composing a letter and planning how to sneak it out of the house to post.

Lady Stanley set the letter aside. "The steward goes on to ask for your patience for he would not be so bold as to arrange a reunion without speaking first to the grieving heir, especially when he does not know the true extent of the man's accumulated and recent injuries. For obvious reasons the wedding will need to be postponed to a later date."

Their wedding is the furthest thing from her mind.

Just Nicholas.

Injured, orphaned Nicholas.

Dear God, grant him comfort.

"Such a tragedy and such unfortunate timing..." Her stepmother touched a fingertip to her still dry eyes in an affectation of sympathy.

Susannah glanced at the others, but they seemed equally unaffected by the news. Then again, they did not know the Penningtons.

"How well did you know this Sir Thomas? Had you visited his estate often?" Lady Stanley smoothed a delicate hand over her skirts.

Susannah stared at her hands in her lap as tears blurred her vision. "Honestly, I knew Sir Thomas more by sight in the area. I only met him once when I was twelve at Muncaster Castle for the celebration bestowing his baronetcy. However, Father met with him at least quarterly in Ravenglass to discuss business."

Why was she so emotional over a man she did not know well? Except after reading his letter each night for the past few weeks, the man had become somewhat of a father figure.

And his tragic death would affect Nicholas even more.

After years of trying to live up to his father's expectations and finally returning home, she could only imagine the devastation to not receive comfort or closure in their reunion. For while Nicholas would be glad to be ransomed, without that circumstance, his father would never have been on the docks for the thieves to target...

Helplessly, she tangled her fingers together in her apron. Whatever could she say to lift that burden?

"And the new baronet—Sir Nicholas—when was the last time you saw him?" Her stepmother's prying words sent prickles of warning up Susannah's spine.

She weighed her response but could not avoid the truth. "I saw him last the day before he set to sea ten years ago."

"So, you were a mere child." She smiled at her girls. "We'll give him time to grieve, but there's no reason not to prepare a wedding gown or trousseau for our Susan."

Susan sat up tall. "Me?"

Lady Stanley waved the letter once again. "Susan. Susannah. Such an easy mistake to make..." She shrugged delicately and aimed a weak smile at Susannah.

However, even as she was dismissed to fetch tea for the others before resuming her laundry duties, Susannah had more than a creeping thought that her stepmother would try to push her daughter to impersonate the true bride.

To steal her betrothal.

But such a plan would never work. For once her Nicholas met the family, the ruse would be exposed.

~Early November

With Stefan breathing heavily beside him, Nicholas slowed his walking pace even more as they made their way toward the docks.

At least the air was not as stifling as a few months ago.

As near as he could recall, it had been almost fourteen weeks since their arrival, making it now early November. But then again, he didn't even know what day of the week it was. Just that the weather was still much warmer than Cumbria would be this time of year.

He glanced at Stefan and the dark circles under his eyes in a pale face that belied the man's heritage. Nicholas had feared a contagion except none of the other slaves had taken ill. Stefan in turn claimed his father had a weak heart with the same signs.

If only the man could rest...

"I worry about you."

"I am in God's hands." A smile flitted around the man's lips. "When I cannot sleep, I have been in prayer. If the Almighty allowed my capture, He must also have a purpose for this moment."

Nicholas shook his head. "I cannot imagine what purpose there is to lose your family and be a slave in a foreign country."

Stefan coughed several times before continuing. "I have to trust that my Savior has a plan and never left me... Is able to deliver me. But even if He does not, like the Hebrew boys in the fiery furnace, I will trust... There is good to come from my life here."

"You're a better man that I am." Nicholas sighed. "But maybe that is because my life has already been a series of perpetual pain. First, I lost my mother, then was sent away from home. But before I could return and earn my father's favor, I was impressed into the Royal Navy where I've had almost ten years of conflict at sea with the nightmares to show for it. I was captured by the French and escaped, only a week later to end up captured again and now a slave." His voice rose along with his temper. "I did not do anything to deserve this."

Stefan's eyes held understanding...and pity. "I know. It is one reason why I pray each night. However, one thing I have learned is that even in captivity, I cannot remain a prisoner to my emotions. I hold the key to let myself find freedom and peace. Even if my body is not my own, I can choose to live freely."

Nicholas blinked. He had been thinking something similar lately. That he needed to win the battle of his mind.

That bitterness was only stealing his strength.

As they turned the final corner toward their destination, Stefan spoke again. "I have been remembering the old stories of those who were also sold or carried away into captivity."

Nicholas glanced around at the vague mention of the Scriptures. They had already been pressured by their captors to convert and therefore spoke only in general terms.

"Joseph faced injustice but somehow remained true to his faith even in the darkness. Until eventually he knew that what man meant for evil, the Almighty used for good."

If only Nicholas could have stayed so true. And yet... "Joseph was destined to be the leader of a nation."

"And you are a Navy officer and a knight with an estate to run. Others depend on you and I do not believe the Almighty is done with you yet... Or me."

Could it be possible?

For the first time in weeks, Nicholas felt the stirring of hope.

Please, God, if there is a way home...

Once the warehouse was in sight, all talk of their faith ceased and under Assad's supervision, they resumed their usual routine of loading crates onto the wagon. Even if lately Stefan did the organizing and Nicholas did most of the heavier lifting.

Despite being enslaved, at least he had his health and strength.

As Nicholas secured the last crate of the load, he heard their taskmaster grumbling near the door as he looked outside for someone.

Only then did he realize that the pair of natives who transported the wagon to the ships were late.

A few moments later, the younger of the two arrived in a panic. Although he spoke frantically in another language, his gestures were clear. Someone needed to deliver the crates, but the boy could not do it alone.

Was it possible they could see more than this warehouse today?

After a pointed glance at Stefan, Nicholas stood near the loaded wagon with his head down as if he was submissively awaiting orders.

Assad stomped closer, then with a fierce frown pointed for them to go with the young man for the delivery. A glare, waving fist, and a hand on his whip promised harsh retribution if they took advantage of their time away from the warehouse.

Nicholas nodded. Out of the corner of his eye, he saw Stefan do the same.

As tempting as it was, they would do nothing to misuse the trust placed in them. For if they even twitched, a beating was assured. Or worse to be sold to a galley.

Their new supervisor thumped his chest and announced his name—Hassim—before pocketing a list from Assad, pointing them to places beside the wagon to steady the cargo, and hitching up the donkey.

Soon they were on their way from the warehouse to the docks where various ships were anchored. Hassim referred to his list, then stopped near a merchant ship flying a Greek flag.

Ever curious, Nicholas took a quick glance at the flags on other ships, spotting some from European countries including Spain and Italy. Along with a few pirate ships and other Barbary nation allies.

Hassim began issuing orders as if he were happy to see grown white slaves obeying him. Moments later, he and Stefan were unloading and carrying crates up the ramp.

At the top, a member of the ship's crew took the list from Hassim and compared the cargo to his own paperwork before directing them on where to put it. Nicholas and Stefan unloaded the wagon to create a stack on the ship's deck while Hassim and a few of the ship's crew carried the crates below deck to the hold.

Nicholas set out to work faster in order to garner favor with the ship's crew and aimed to have all the crates on the deck quickly so that Hassim would be more likely to give a favorable report.

Stefan moved slower but still did his fair share.

Once, when their paths crossed near the wagon, Stefan grinned. "Could it be we have found favor with the jailer?"

Nicholas raised his eyebrows at the question, then puzzled over the implications as they worked. If they found favor, would they be granted more freedom?

Once the last crates were unloaded onto the ship's deck, they returned and stood by the empty wagon. Hassim waved at the crew member with the list and jogged down the ramp to join them and lead them back to the warehouse.

Assad met them wide-eyed at the door to the warehouse. Whatever was said in his rapid exchange with Hassim must have been good, for he almost smiled at Nicholas and Stefan before waving them toward a new pile of crates to load onto the wagon.

Stefan battled a coughing fit as they worked, but found enough breath to chuckle. "There once was a young prince whose brothers sold him into slavery in Egypt. He worked diligently for his master until he eventually was placed in charge of the household."

Nicholas fought a smile for Stefan was back to talking about Joseph again. "I remember that story. But someone lied and he got thrown in prison."

Stefan had a twinkle in his eye as he reached for another crate. "And there he worked diligently for his new master until he was placed in charge of everything. Then one day, when the time was right, an opportunity came and he was suddenly raised to the palace."

"I don't think we have such an outcome in our future." He had yet to see a true palace in this port town.

"You have a castle, do you not?"

Nicholas rolled his eyes as he loaded the last crate onto the wagon, but took it to heart to work diligently just like Joseph.

After another warning glare from Assad, they were sent back out with Hassim to a different ship, this one from Italy.

Except while delivering crates up a ramp onto the deck under the watchful eye of another crew member, something happened.

A crate-filled net being transferred from the dock area to an adjacent ship's hold broke free from the rope and pulley system. And collided with the railing, damaging that ship, injuring men, and spreading chaos. Amidst the shouts for help and sailors running everywhere including their ramp's keeper and Hassim, others took advantage of the mayhem to loot the damaged cargo including a few who even jumped into the water.

And at the end of a string of galley slaves being led toward a distant ship, one somehow broke free, swung his chains at his keeper, and tried to disappear into the crowd only to be brought down violently by that same keeper.

Fear of a similar fate kept Nicholas' feet temporarily anchored in place, but he saw no fewer than a half dozen opportunities to disappear into the water, into the hold, or to slip behind the piles of barrels and goods waiting to be loaded.

If he had been a different or more desperate man, he could already be free.

Was it possible? Could he risk it?

Not yet.

He needed to plan for contingencies, especially to get Stefan safely away with him and for them to avoid discovery until far from Morocco.

He forced himself to resume his earlier task unloading the wagon onto the ship as if nothing had happened. Hassim's surprise to find them still present upon his return was reward enough.

But Nicholas could tell from Stefan's occasional glance at the piles of cargo and the trapdoor to the ship's hold that his friend had seen the same opportunities. If they continued to have access to the ships, there might come a day when escape was possible.

Over the course of the long day, he and Stefan helped deliver crates to or collected deliveries from five different ships. So, by the time they walked back to the bagnio to sleep, he was both exhausted and exhilarated. Especially with the fresh realization of how close he was to other ships and how many places there were to hide onboard.

Beside him, Stefan bent over with another coughing fit. One that resulted in blood on his lips and even slower steps to go with his gray pallor.

Nicholas wrapped an arm around the man's waist to lend him strength. "I was glad for today's change but fear it was too much for you."

"Everything is too much for me... And every day brings me one step closer to eternity." Stefan paused to catch his breath. "I fear I will not survive for long... But I want my life to count for something."

Later, when they had claimed their sleeping mats on the hard ground, Stefan gripped Nicholas' hand. "I don't think I'm ever going to see my homeland again. There is nothing there for me there after losing my family." He shook his head. "However, you have told me of your home enough that if there is ever a chance, I will help you slip onboard."

Hope warred with fear in his chest.

Stefan's eyes blazed in the dim light of a nearby candle. "Just promise you'll make the most of the remainder of your life."

That was a heavy burden, especially when all he wanted was a simple life in the country with a garden to plant. But to assure his friend, he nodded.

Chapter Eight

Mid November, a shout from the ground level drew Susannah away from her task of organizing Susan's wardrobe on the second floor. She quickly moved to the banister to eavesdrop, then leaned over just enough to spot her stepmother waving a letter as Susan and Pru appeared in the doorway to the drawing room.

"Girls, we will have a very special visitor tomorrow. Sir Nicholas Pennington."

Her heart leapt in her chest.

It had been six weeks since the Muncaster steward's note. Obviously Nicholas was recovered enough to travel, but why would he come here to reeking Liverpool? Unless the late baronet's merchant routes...

"He writes that he has other business to attend to in town but plans to pay a call to become reacquainted."

Giddy squeals erupted with a flurried discussion of dresses and refreshments that grew faint as they apparently retreated back into the room.

Reacquainted? Dread pooled in her gut.

Nicholas had never met her stepmother, which meant the woman was stealing her mail again.

A flash of anger propelled Susannah down the stairs. "Hand it over at once."

Her stepmother blocked the doorway and held the letter out of reach. "It was addressed to Miss Stanley, who of course is properly the eldest daughter in the household." She smirked and turned her head to call over her shoulder. "Susan, it is time for you to become acquainted with your future husband."

Bile rose in Susannah's throat at the realization that her suspicions were well founded. But Nicholas was her only escape out of this household.

She lifted her chin. "Nicholas is betrothed to *me*. Susannah Stanley." And she had a copy of the agreement to prove it.

"Susan. Susannah. Anna." Lady Stanley waved a hand over Susannah's attire. "You have a similar look, but only one of you is dressed the part of a knight's daughter."

Susannah glanced down at her worn dress with the stains on the skirt. With the exception of her dress for Pru's debut which was too fancy for a simple tea, the remainder of her wardrobe was in a similar state.

Nevertheless...

"He will know the difference. It might have been ten years but there are things only we know about our time together." She glared over her stepmother's shoulder at the would-be sister who had joined them. "You did not grow up in our valley and only lived at Dalegarth Hall a few months. He *will* know you are an impostor."

Doubt flashed in Susan's eyes before she glanced at her mother.

Lady Stanley only sneered. "How? You have grown and changed since I first met you. And by your own admission, it has been even longer since he laid eyes on you. Any lapses of memory about past events can easily be excused by the passage of time."

Doubt must be contagious. For while she bore the scar and treasured the remnants of fur, was it possible that he could have forgotten about her? No. His letter acknowledging their betrothal referenced the event that brought them together.

She almost blurted out the details of that memorable day, but bit her tongue. She could not give them ammunition in this war for her freedom.

Her stepmother must have taken her temporary silence as a sign for she smiled. "Of course, as your dear mama, I will be right there beside you to show proper outrage that my own flesh and blood would try to impersonate my late husband's child." She fluttered her eyelashes as if innocent of subterfuge.

A chill ran down Susannah's spine. The woman could be charming when she wished and a lesser man might believe her facade.

"Do not defy me or I will have you committed to an asylum before the week is done."

Icy cold tentacles of fear squeezed her chest.

Dear God, help me...

No. She had to believe that Nicholas was not a lesser man.

If he did not immediately spot the differences himself, she would simply bring up a mention of the Dalegarth waterfall in casual conversation and see where that led.

"I am sure you will make the right choice." The dreadful woman smiled as if nothing were amiss, then gestured toward the back of the house. "Once you have completed your regular chores, please be sure we have fresh tea cakes to serve to our illustrious guest."

Susannah retreated to inventory the kitchen while relieved that the drawing room had been cleaned just that morning. Susan could see to her own clothing. In the meantime, her mind spun with possible questions that could reveal the truth once Nicholas was in their midst.

But come dawn as she was dressing for the day, she heard a rustle outside her door and a metallic click.

No. It couldn't be.

She rushed over but the door was locked from the outside.

She rattled the knob, then yanked on the door. "Let me out! You can't do this."

A low chuckle came from the other side. "I am so sorry that you aren't feeling well, Anna. Perhaps you should stay in your room and rest today..."

"No!" Her voice cracked. "You cannot keep me in here."

The woman snorted. "It will be a hardship to be without your services, but under the circumstances, I have no other choice." The sound of footsteps retreated in the hall outside.

Susannah continued to pound on the door and shouted loudly for help. Perhaps the others in the household would hear her and have mercy.

By midday, with bruised hands and an aching throat, it was clear no one would be coming to her rescue.

She sank to the floor and leaned against the door. Her stomach cramped with hunger and she had already resorted to drinking the little water in the pitcher at her washstand to replace her tears.

Oh God, why? First my mother and brother. Then Nicholas, my new friend and rescuer, was gone and impressed. My father...

Suddenly she recalled the image of her father's broken body lying in the rain on the very trail where Nicholas had safely cradled her home to cozy Dalegarth Hall.

Another sob shook her shoulders.

She had lost her family, inheritance, and identity. And now, a future with her hero was slipping through her fingers and there was nothing she could do about it.

The lyrics of a familiar lament about other women who had lost their men in battle welled up and she began to sing. "We'll hae nae mair lilting, at the yowe-milking, women and bairns are dowie and wae. Sighing and moaning, on ilka green loaning, the flowers of the forest are all wede away."

As the last note echoed in her small room on the top floor, she sagged back against the door and stared out her tiny window at the gray skies.

Emptied of all emotion, she vaguely registered the sounds of activity on the street. And closer, doors opening and closing.

Feminine laughter and a deeper voice.

Weakened by her relentless tears and the lack of food, she curled into a ball on the cold floor, afraid to hope for a miracle.

If her stepmother's scheme succeeded, there was nothing left for her.

Time passed by with more doors opening and closing and even later another male voice followed by laughter.

And still no one came to let her out.

Was she in need of additional punishment simply for believing in the truth of her heritage as Sir William's daughter?

Oh, Father, how I wish you were here.

As the shadows stretched across her floor, footsteps approached and she shakily rose to her feet.

The lock clicked and the door swung open to reveal her stepmother beaming a satisfied but wicked smile. "Your Nicholas is a charming man and it is all arranged. The groom is convinced of our sincerity and could not take his eyes off our dear Susan."

A fresh wave of betrayal stabbed her heart. For apparently her betrothed did not care enough to spot their duplicity. Had he changed so much?

Lady Stanley lifted her chin. "In fact, he agreed that a wedding would be the perfect way to start the new year and insisted that we hold the ceremony here in Liverpool with our friends in attendance."

So soon after losing his father? And yet, at least the banns would not be read that week. Gifting her with time to stop the impersonation.

Perhaps a visit to the cathedral for a confession was in order...

The woman raised an eyebrow. "However, lest you get any ideas of protesting once the banns are read, the happy couple has already been to speak to Bishop Langley about their intentions."

The bishop. Who had ever only known her as Anna.

That spark of hope dwindled.

"Now that your day of leisure is complete, it is time to resume your duties to this family. After all, there is a yet an empty tea tray in the drawing room and someone must prepare the evening meal." Her stepmother looked down her nose in disgust, before turning and sweeping out of sight.

A day of leisure?

She had not had one of those in years.

However, eager to escape the confines of her room, Susannah did not protest the woman's orders as she descended the stairs in her wake.

Immediate access to the kitchen would allow her to alleviate her hunger and thirst. And she was already thinking of an empty crock she could fill with water to store in her room along with some sort of foodstuffs.

After today, the chances of being locked in her room again would only increase as the wedding drew nigh.

The same wedding she had dreamed of for years as a distraction from her grief and loneliness.

And now Nicholas had failed her too.

Bitterness clawed inside her chest.

And yet maybe when he saw her in attendance at the wedding, he would recognize his error and make his own protests...

Another dim spark of hope ignited.

Ten years was a long time, and since her previous letters to Ravenglass had been blocked, he might not know about her current situation or stepsisters.

Letters that had been blocked by the same woman who arranged the current ruse. And one who was more likely to imprison Susannah once again than allow her to attend the wedding.

She tripped over suddenly clumsy feet.

Would her prison be the room abovestairs?

Or Bedlam as threatened?

Why did the woman even keep her around? For free labor or for something else?

No matter. She could not bear to continue living under the same roof and needed to develop a plan of escape.

While the language difference was still a barrier to understanding, apparently the regular delivery driver was not able to return. Because after two weeks of Nicholas and Stefan loading the wagon and then going with Hassim to the docks to make the deliveries or following his orders to then fill the wagon with crates from a different ship, one day the young man was nowhere in sight.

Instead, Assad handed Nicholas a sheet of parchment with a dock number and ship name at the top, then waved them out the door with the full wagon as if he were now eliminating the middleman and pocketing more of the profits.

It had been the hardest thing Nicholas had ever done not to abuse that trust as they found the correct ship and completed the delivery of goods.

Assad's smile at their return with the signed invoice was reward enough. Their master apparently thought they were docile or dumb but that could only work to their benefit later.

During their walk back to the bagnio that evening, Stefan praised the providence of God for granting them favor and began quietly discussing the best time for a diversion.

By the time they arrived at the warehouse the next morning, they had concluded that once the right ship was found, the delivery had to be completed and the invoice signed so the ship's crew had no reason to pay attention to Nicholas any longer. In fact, if Nicholas could start down the ramp, even better. Because if questioned, the crew would believe that he had left and disappeared somewhere on the crowded docks instead of slipping back onboard.

And if Stefan was in possession of the signed invoice, he might be able to avoid punishment while claiming ignorance about where Nicholas had disappeared to.

He argued hard against leaving Stefan with the risk of reprisal, but the man had a gleam in his eye. And even claimed he might decide to carry his diversion all the way onboard a different ship and let God deliver him if He so chose.

While Nicholas continued to be faithful in his duties, prayers for liberation rose heavenward at increasing intervals. At times guilt pinched his conscience as he planned to betray Assad's trust if given the chance, and yet, wasn't he a soldier with the duty to escape?

A week later, his opportunity came in the form of a Turkish ship being loaded with cargo to trade in Spain.

Only one sailor stood at the top of the ramp to check the list of cargo being delivered onboard. The ship's purser seemed more interested in scratching his paunch and yawning as if he had overindulged in the crew's celebratory night at port before setting to sea than paying attention to the white slaves delivering the cargo.

To test his theory, Nicholas carried one crate onto the deck but then lingered near the open hold where two other slovenly crew members lowered the crates. He caught a glimpse of a decrepit ladder and disorderly piles below before stepping back.

His pulse hammered.

Not only was the ship sailing within the hour for a destination allied with the English, but his chances of stowing away below decks were good. No one on this crew would notice a bit of missing food or a change of clothing.

He masked his expression and turned down the ramp for another crate. As he passed Stefan going up, he caught his eye and nodded.

As they crossed paths on the return trip, his friend nodded back.

The time had come to place their fates in the hands of the Almighty.

Nicholas deliberately slowed his steps so as not to draw attention to himself with a change in behavior. A few minutes later, he delivered the last crate while Stefan paused beside the ramp guard to receive the signed invoice.

Nicholas set the crate down near the ladder, then paused to stretch his back muscles while keeping an eye on the purser who never glanced his way.

"Godspeed in your journeys, my friend." Stefan executed a half bow as if speaking to the crewman, tucked the paper inside his shirt, and started down the ramp.

Nicholas stilled. They had never discussed what type of diversion his friend had planned so he was surprised when the man stopped in the middle of the boards and burst into a violent coughing fit.

It was so convincing, he almost spoiled his chance of escape by rushing to his friend's side.

Until one cough sounded suspiciously like the name Joseph and another like the word castle. A moment later, Stefan bent over and accidentally slipped from the ramp and fell into the water below with a giant splash.

The shouts of a man overboard drew even the loading crew members to the railing as they lowered ropes to rescue the drowning slave.

With another prayer for God's favor, Nicholas clambered down the ladder into the ship's hold and darted out of sight behind a pile of crates. His location took him closer to an abandoned gunport.

It was indeed a blessing in that he would have fresh air and a bit of daylight. Then through the half-opened portal, he spotted a dripping Stefan shivering on the quay and leading the donkey-pulled wagon in the opposite direction of their master's warehouse.

As footsteps echoed overhead, Nicholas whispered, "Godspeed in your journeys as well, my friend."

He crouched down behind the crates and waited.

Once the rest of the cargo was lowered from the deck, he watched as the crew replaced the deck cover concealing the hold. As his eyes adjusted to the dim lighting, he spied barrels of fresh water and baskets of foodstuffs near a doorway which must lead to the galley and crew quarters. As well as a canvas bag with items of clothing hanging out.

God had provided for all his needs.

While the crew was busy overhead preparing to set sail—per the shouts and clanking of an anchor chain being raised—Nicholas changed from his slave rags into an ill-fitting shirt and trousers, then retreated with a light meal to his porthole corner to wait.

Once they were underway, he breathed even easier.

And not even a sudden storm in the middle of the crossing could sour his mood for every mile brought him closer to land.

Within the week, they arrived at their first destination. Once some of the cargo had been unloaded, many of the crew seemed to have made for shore leaving a grumbling few behind to stand watch.

Rather than risk detection in the main corridors, Nicholas waited for cover of darkness and then lowered himself from the gunport before dropping into the frigid waters.

He stayed close to the hull long enough to confirm he had not been heard, then quietly swam across the harbor for the distant shore.

Exhausted, he pulled himself out of the water and found a hiding place to await the sun. But despite the bone-shaking shivers caused by wet clothing and the impending winter weather, he had never felt so happy to be free.

Once morning dawned, he foraged for food on the outskirts of the small town, then began his long journey north. He might have to cross hundreds of miles with untold dangers around every bend, but the hardest part was behind him. Eventually he was sure to come across an English patrol or a naval vessel anchored in a harbor.

He had been given a second chance at life and he wasn't about to waste God's gift or Stefan's sacrifice.

And with a girl's stalwart belief that he could do anything if he put his mind to it, he embraced whatever challenges came his way.

God, after ten long years, please bring me home.

Part Two

Chapter Nine

The late December chill soaked into Susannah's aching bones as their wagon rattled over the rutted road toward Ravenglass and the castle not far beyond.

Along with Mr. Kendall, the middle-aged man hired to drive the team and do the heavy lifting, she had been sent to Muncaster a week before the wedding with orders to unpack the multitude of trunks secured under a piece of weathered canvas behind her. In addition to setting Susan's bedchamber and dressing room to rights for when she returned from her honeymoon, she was also to speak to the housekeeper about Susan's likes and dislikes.

To help ease her transition into married life in a strange place.

In the very region Susan had once been so eager to escape.

The place Susannah had eagerly longed to return to.

Except this homecoming wasn't at all like she had imagined. For the few glimpses of the Eskdale valley she'd captured between the roadside trees had stirred memories of her dead parents...and those of a heroic rescue.

Had her childish naiveté-imposed character qualities upon a boy that he did not possess?

A shiver of foreboding that had nothing to do with the damp weather and icy temperatures swept down her spine.

Too soon the hired man pulled their wagon to a halt outside the door of Muncaster Castle. After being helped down from her perch and discretely working feeling back into her stiff legs, she claimed her overfilled valise from behind the seat.

Everything she owned—what little indeed—was inside, but she could not risk leaving anything of value behind to be discovered or destroyed in her absence.

God willing, she would never return to Liverpool.

At the door, they were greeted by a stern butler she did not recognize and Mr. Kendall handed over a letter of introduction.

As the butler read the missive, his eyes widened before a sneer curled his lips and heat flooded her face. Most likely he had discovered she had been traveling alone with a man who was not her husband.

Little did he know her stepmother's travel arrangements were the least of Susannah's concerns.

Moments later, the butler showed them inside an entryway that bore sparse decorations for the Christmas season. The space was warmer than out-of-doors but felt cold and gloomy, so very unlike the last time she had set foot in this place on a happier occasion and in the summer.

Then again, the current household was still in mourning and laughter or smiles from the staff would be inappropriate even if Twelfth Night was days away.

The butler directed them where to put the trunks and soon Susannah followed Mr. Kendall up the stairs. But as she ventured down the corridor toward their destination, she could not help but believe the ancient castle was in need of a thorough refreshing if not redecorating.

Something was missing, for it did not feel like a home.

She entered the designated door and was pleasantly surprised to find a lavish suite decorated with the greens and golds of the valley and well-built furniture. Susan might not have picked the colors, but even with a seating area near the windows, she should also appreciate the attached private sitting room with its own door to the hallway.

Susannah had opened the first trunk and was beginning to think about where to put the many gowns when she finally registered the lack of men's clothing in the dressing room. And the lack of personal touches elsewhere.

Unless the butler had directed them to the wrong room, this suite was for Susan alone.

Why did high society couples feel the need for separate living quarters instead of sharing their lives completely like her parents had?

Her stomach soured with a new realization. Even if Nicholas had somehow recognized Susannah as his rightful bride to be, he apparently had no desire to share a room with his wife.

She wrestled her feelings of rejection into submission even while a traitorous part of her heart wondered where his rooms were located.

If he was sequestered in his study at that very moment.

Or most likely miles away.

For despite weeks of vicious threats of locking her away permanently for her alleged delusions, if her stepmother went to these lengths to get Susannah out of Liverpool so she could not possibly protest the wedding, then the woman must also know that the groom would not be here.

Which meant the current task had a dual purpose to punish Susannah by letting her get close to her dreams of a loving home...while knowing it was forever out of her reach.

Mr. Kendall deposited the last trunk near the others in the middle of the room and dusted off his hands. "I wish you well, miss." With a dip of his head, he disappeared out the door.

Leaving her alone in the room...and stranded in Ravenglass? Her hands shook.

While she had hoped to never return south, she had assumed her stepmother had made other arrangements. Although, perhaps those were stated in the letter given to the butler. Would it be impertinent to ask?

In the meantime, she had a task to accomplish.

Over the next hour, she emptied the trunks and put all of Susan's things away. She would have arranged additional items on the dressing table, except those were needed by the bride this week and later on her wedding trip.

Bitterness roiled at the injustice and she pressed a hand over her stomach.

God, why would You allow such a thing to happen to me?

Perhaps she should make her own way back south in time to stop the sham wedding after all.

An austere woman in a plain black gown entered the room and glanced around. She nodded as if relieved to find Susannah had not damaged the furnishings, then turned narrowed eyes her direction. "You must be Anna."

"I'm actually Sus—"

"Your mistress called you Anna and so shall I." The woman waved a letter that looked thicker than the one Mr. Kendall had given to the butler.

"Mistress?" Surely this woman was confused, except the name Anna... Susannah straightened her skirts and lifted her chin. "And you are..." She raised an eyebrow and waited.

The woman huffed. "I am Mrs. Finch, the housekeeper newly charged with the task to set the current staff to rights. However, as much as Lady Stanley wishes you to be appointed lady's maid, you will have to prove yourself to me first."

Lady's maid?

Susannah blinked away sudden tears at the revelation that her stepmother never intended for her to return to Liverpool at all but truly wished for an extended punishment by continuing to serve Susan.

Why did the woman hate her so?

A hollow feeling grew around her heart as the truth finally sank in. Susannah had no family anymore.

Meanwhile, Mrs. Finch rambled on about a maid's uniform, a possible shared room in the basement if another girl agreed, and duties as a scullery maid with the possibility of advancement before her indenture expired.

Indenture?

Susannah gasped. "I am the daughter of a knight, not a servant—"

"She wrote that you would try to put on airs as if you were ever more than a maid." Mrs. Finch muttered something, then waved the letter in her hand. "I have the papers right here. Your remaining two years have been signed over to the baronet as a wedding gift."

Any such papers were an obvious forgery as well as a malicious lie to bind her to this fate without recourse from the authorities. And now, instead of his bride, she was his slave?

Susannah clenched her fists as hot tears burned her eyes. What name was written on the papers? And had Nicholas—Sir Nicholas—even seen them before his departure?

"Come along." Mrs. Finch pivoted toward the door.

Susannah grabbed her valise and followed the housekeeper down rambling hallways until they reached the kitchen where she was promptly introduced to Mrs. Jennings as the new scullery maid.

"Do not give her any leeway since she's indentured." Mrs. Finch waved that dreadful paper once again. "See that she receives a proper uniform and give her a cot in the storeroom until Edith makes room." With another huff, she swept from the room.

The cook glared at the now empty doorway and Susannah recalled the housekeeper's words about the current staff. It seemed she might have a potential ally in the making, but must tread cautiously.

Mrs. Jennings turned her attention to Susannah, eying her garments up and down. Though worn and secondhand, her dress revealed quality above that of a servant. "What is your name?"

"Sus—" The threats of an asylum and the reality of indenture papers stole her voice. She swallowed hard. "They call me Anna, ma'am."

"Where are you from?" Mrs. Jennings narrowed her eyes as she studied Susannah's face.

She resisted the urge to squirm under the scrutiny. She could not tell the truth but could not bear to lie either. "I was born here in the Lake District, but Liverpool has been home for the last five years."

"And your parents?"

She swallowed again, this time tasting her tears. "Dead."

The woman nodded, then quickly set about locating a dull gray dress and pointing Susannah to the storeroom to change clothes and store her valise. Mere minutes later, Susannah was hard at work chopping vegetables and scouring pots.

She was glad for the task because busy hands meant less time to ponder her lost dreams. And equally relieved that outside the presence of the stern housekeeper and butler, the remainder of the staff she met seemed the friendly sort, full of chatter and gossip especially as they gathered for their evening meal.

From their animated conversations, it was immediately confirmed that the lord of the castle was not at home.

Even if she dared venture upstairs again, there was no one to see. Leaving her no choice but to accept the fact that within days her childhood hero would be irrevocably married to another.

However, she also noticed their frowns and other comments about how he hadn't been the same since his return. How he seemed to have left his good humor on the continent. That he was quick tempered and a recluse. And how he had not left the castle grounds except for business when as a boy he used to roam the countryside at will.

According to those who knew him now, Sir Nicholas Pennington was nothing like the man living in her imagination.

Which meant that her two fictional years of servitude might be a small price to pay to have escaped a lifetime of a different sort of bondage to a man tainted by his war experiences.

But their mention of his former countryside ramblings ignited a desire to explore.

She leaned forward to address the cook at the other end of the table. "Will I have any free time?"

Mrs. Jennings shrugged. "The regular staff gets a half day every other week, but I do not know if the same applies to indentured servants."

Susannah felt the distancing disdain from the others around the table and shrank back from their prejudice.

"Why would you ask?" Mrs. Jennings frowned. "Are you thinking to escape your obligation?"

She quickly weighed her words. "You mentioned the countryside and the little I saw on my travels here intrigued me. Liverpool did not have the open spaces I enjoyed in my youth. And I still have a distant cousin who lives in..." She barely stopped herself from mentioning Boot for it edged too close to the truth. "I cannot recall. But didn't—" The name stuck in her throat and she coughed. "Did not the soon-to-be Lady Pennington once live somewhere near here?"

Others thankfully picked up the conversation about the small village of Boot. And how the only redeeming feature now was their waterfall, especially since Mr. Stanley abandoned Dalegarth Hall and moved down the coast.

Susannah tried to mask her shock but failed. "Why would someone abandon a hall?"

"Money."

"I heard that the lavish bequests in the late Sir William's will bankrupted the coffers. What good is a home without an income?"

"I wonder if the new mistress of the house will mourn the demise of her childhood home?"

"She had seemed like such a sweet girl the few times I saw her with her father in town."

Susan as sweet? And missing Boot?

Susannah snorted at the thought, then quickly tried to mask her reaction with a cough. But Mrs. Jennings' astute gaze pinned her in place.

She would have to try for another topic deflection. "Well, if visiting the area is out of the question, what about church services?"

She quickly learned that while services were still held at St. Michael's church on the Muncaster grounds, the Reverend Brooks from her youth had been promoted to bishop serving the Deanery of Calder in the Dioceses of Carlile.

Leaving the relatively new Reverend Edwards in his place.

A man she had never met and one who would be ill-suited to stop the impending wedding even if there were time.

Susannah finished the remainder of her meal in silence, trapped in her thoughts as securely as she was trapped within the castle grounds for the foreseeable future with no contact with anyone from her past and only a distant view of her beloved valley to keep her company.

She would simply have to bide her time in bitter servitude until the opportunity came to forge a new path for her future.

was abovestairs filling the pitchers, I heard the master berating his valet and when I passed her in the hall, I thought I saw bruises on her arms and tears on her face."

"Silence." Mrs. Jennings' voice echoed brought all activity to a halt. "There is enough to be done without unnecessary gossip in my kitchen."

Scolded, the staff returned to their tasks, but Susannah could not ignore the frown on the cook's face. Or the image of abuse Edith's words had portrayed.

They said Sir Nicholas had not been the same since his return from war. And while she knew Susan's selfishness could provoke anyone, based on the underlying tension all day, others had surely felt the man's lash of anger before.

At some point she was sure to encounter him and prayed he did not cause a scene.

Susannah was in the midst of carrying china plates piled with warm tea cakes toward the trays when Mrs. Finch entered the room and all activity stopped.

The woman's critical gaze swept the room, then paused with a severe frown as her eyes lit upon Susannah. "Lady Pennington has specifically requested that Anna deliver her tea."

Her stomach dropped. There was no avoiding the first confrontation now.

And no ignoring the surrounding looks of speculation, jealousy, and suspicion. As if she were a spy planted ahead of time to test their loyalties and report to the mistress.

If only they knew the true deceiver...

She nodded her acceptance to the housekeeper, then lowered the plates to the trays with shaking hands.

A minute later, she followed a footman out of the kitchen praying her legs would hold her to her destination. While she had not ventured outside the kitchen since the day she arrived with Susan's trunks, at least she knew where to go.

However, when she turned the corner of the hallway on the second floor, she almost ran into a tall finely-dressed gentleman with brown hair.

He scanned her person, then sneered at the scar on her inner arm. Except due to her grip on the tray, she could do nothing to hide from the blatant scrutiny in his cold amber eyes.

Only avert her eyes as becoming a proper servant and wish for the humor and warm compassion she'd once seen in a different pair of dark brown eyes.

Had Sir Nicholas brought another companion or guest into his home? The servants' grapevine had been silent on that account.

"Step aside, you hideous wench." The man's scathing order sent a chill down her spine. "In the future, keep your scarred limbs out of sight. My castle deserves only the best even in my servants."

His castle?

She numbly nodded, then moved out of his way as he continued down the corridor leaving her standing alone on shaking limbs.

Dear God, who was that man? Because he is not Nicholas.

Tears pricked her eyes.

Whatever had happened to the real Nicholas?

And why hadn't the servants seen the difference? Surely they had noticed more than his change in behavior? And yet, who would believe her claims now especially when her own true identity must be concealed upon threat of Bedlam?

If only Sir Thomas had not perished on the docks before—

She gasped. Wouldn't a father know his own son?

No. That possibility was too horrifying to consider.

All she knew was that if she had indeed been allowed in the room for the reunion with the long-gone soldier instead of locked away, there never would have been a wedding.

And Susan would never have taken her place.

Susan.

Suddenly remembering the tray and the cooling tea, Susannah hurried onward to the rooms of the woman who had stolen her identity.

But if she reclaimed her name, would their marriage be void...or would she herself be forced to take Susan's place as if married by proxy?

She shuddered to think of the coldness in that man's eyes.

God had truly spared her such a fate.

She needed to pray about the future and make plans to get far away from here. Or should she try to reveal the truth for the real Nicholas' sake? For the sake of the Pennington name?

Her head pounded with the endless questions. Questions she would need to consider later when alone in her basement room.

After balancing the tray on her hip, Susannah knocked on the bedroom door, then quietly entered. Sidestepping the general disarray of scattered items of clothing, she moved to the seating area and placed the tray on the low table.

"Oh, Anna." Susan rushed to her side and fell into her arms, sobbing. "I'm married to a horrid man."

Susannah bit her lip to keep from spilling the truth, and while comforting the distraught woman she took in the very bruises Edith had seen. Almost as if Susan had been shaken or forced aside.

"You must help me, sister."

Sister? It had been years since there had been any sisterly feelings shared between them.

Susannah gently led her to a chair and proceeded to pour a cup of tea as the newlywed ranted about how her husband simply refused to go to London for the season and instead insisted they would be staying in the Lake Country.

"My dreams of going about in society are thwarted at every turn." Susan hiccupped. "What is the point of being a lady if I cannot go anywhere?"

It seemed her selfish nature had not changed one iota.

And while there was never a reason for a gentleman to lay a hand on a woman, let alone his wife, she could understand the impostor's frustrations.

Susan set her half-empty cup aside and proceeded to march about the room. "I could have married a rich man in Liverpool. At least there I would be invited to parties." Her skirts whirled about her as she turned wide eyes on Susannah. "We have to reverse Mother's plan so I can be free to—"

"No!" Susannah took a deep breath to calm herself. "You cannot undo your marriage any more than I can undo her forged indenture papers."

Her stepsister looked down at the carpet but not before Susannah spied the guilt in her eyes.

She suppressed her anger over yet another reminder of how much her so-called family hated her and lifted her chin. The time had come for another dose of truth.

"You are truly married in the eyes of God. Not to mention, all of your *friends* in Liverpool witnessed your wedding. And how many from polite society did you meet in Bath?"

The woman sank back down onto a chair as if finally realizing that in her quest for a titled husband, she had removed her other options. She covered her face with her hands and wailed like a petulant child. "I am well and truly trapped here in the backcountry I hate."

Susannah shook her head. "You knew the location of this castle when you took your vows and now you will have to make the most of it."

"Maybe it would be more tolerable if I had a friend or two." Susan peeked out between her fingers. "If you were my lady's maid then we could spend time together and—"

"No, thank you. I would rather not." It was too little too late for a friendship.

However, she could not deny the twinge of compassion that emerged despite the walls around her heart. Susan was married to a man of uncertain character and she could see the bruises for herself. If the woman continued to complain about something or the other, it would only make things worse.

Susannah sighed. "If you have to stay here for at least this Season, why not make Muncaster a beautiful place where others would want to come visit in the summer months? Perhaps a project like decorating a room or two? Or maybe even a new garden to take your mind off your loneliness? You could hire someone to design—"

"I would have to get his permission first." Susan sat up, then grasped at Susannah's hand. "What should I say...?"

"That's up to you now, Lady Pennington." She tried to rein in her sarcasm. "I am just a humble indentured servant with duties in the kitchens below." She turned for the door and left without waiting to be dismissed.

Chapter Ten

~*March 1814*

Setting one weary foot in front of the other, Nicholas finally neared the end of his journey home. With the village of Ravenglass ahead on the muddy road, he could not help but reflect on the past few months.

After escaping slavery in Morocco, he had worked his way across the poor and war-torn regions of Spain in increasingly colder weather while evading recapture and laboring for enough coin to survive. At long last, he had come upon a British military detail and felt honor-bound to send word to his superiors that he was still alive.

For a few weeks, he feared he would be required to rejoin the Royal Navy or risk punishment as a defector. He shuddered at the memories of war and the nightmares that had eased only slightly in Morocco...only to be replaced with new horrors as a slave.

He lifted his face toward the sun and breathed in the fresh sea air.

Word finally arrived at the British outpost that he had been feared dead after the prison escape in France and that he had since been released from duty with the thanks of a grateful nation.

While glad at the veiled confirmation that at least some of the other escapees had survived, there had been no financial support or assistance offered to see him the rest of the way home. He had felt the slight, then resigned himself to the reality that all their efforts were likely focused on the push into France.

So, after leaving the outpost, he found a Spanish port where English ships sometimes stopped...then labored once again to earn the money for his passage since his letter to his father went unanswered.

God only knew what that might mean for his homecoming reception.

Nicholas passed a sign on the outskirts of Ravenglass and picked up his pace. It had been almost eleven years since he had set sail expecting only to be gone for a year at most.

He glanced around at the changes in the village with more homes and larger trees. However, of it all, he had changed more than they.

Had he finally made his father proud and honored the Pennington name?

He almost tripped over a loose cobblestone, then blamed his hole-ridden boots. Having escaped slavery with only the clothes on his back, he had since managed to accumulate a small bag of spare clothing. But only the necessities, leaving him in rough workman's garb with long hair and a thick beard after not seeing a razor for months.

No matter, for a castle awaited.

He chuckled. If they even remained, his boyhood garments would never fit his current frame. But perhaps his father would overlook such things in the joy of their reunion.

Then again, he could not help but recall the decorum required in the dining room and already felt the stricture of society's rules shackling the relative freedoms he had enjoyed over the past decade.

Seeing the sign for The Fox ahead, he decided to stop by the pub for a meal and information. He needed his strength and perhaps even a strategy before walking the final mile east to Muncaster. After all, his father might be away on business and the townspeople would know.

And the subtle reminder of his past heroics might buoy his courage.

Oh, it was good to be home.

Nicholas entered the dim establishment and chose a table out of the way. A table where visiting fishermen used to sit so hopefully no one would look too closely at his current appearance.

He nodded at the proprietor who brought a bowl of stew and a pint of ale...and did not ask any questions.

In years gone by, their stablemaster—his friend Harold's father—had often invited Nicholas along on trips to Ravenglass, especially when his own father was away on business. And whenever they had stopped by the pub, Mr. Oakley had given the boys malted milk—instead of ale—along with a wink and a smile.

Nicholas grinned at the memories, then took a long pull at his grown-up beverage as he eyed the others in the room. The older set looked generally familiar—including the gray-bearded farmer at the adjacent table—but the few who closer to his age did not. Then again, they would have been mere boys like himself when he'd last had the chance to see them.

A man in fancier clothes than he'd recalled around the village entered and he heard the others greet him as Mr. Ellis. Before he could guess at the man's profession, one patron asked how it was going at Muncaster and another mumbled something about a steward having an easy job.

He sat taller and eyed the stranger.

Had any of his father's letters mentioned a new steward? He only recalled a mention that the faithful Mr. Young was ailing, but then again, mail delivery to a war zone was unreliable and sporadic at best.

However, following along with the steward might be the smoothest way to infiltrate his home.

He shook his head. Years at war had certainly changed him if he still thought in terms of strategies and tactics.

Across the tavern, the castle steward raised his voice and asked the room at large to keep an ear to the ground for anyone looking for work. "I'm requested to find a gardener to update and expand the gardens around Muncaster. The baronet seems to believe that improvements will entice the fashionable set to our district."

Since when did his father wish to entice the same people he used to call pretentious snobs?

The farmer closest to Nicholas scoffed. "Sir Thomas, were he still alive, would never stand for such pageantry."

Were he still alive?

Nicholas' heart stopped, then pounded in his chest.

His father was dead?

He cleared his throat to mask the emotion and turned to the men. "I've been away too long if I missed that news. How long ago did Sir Thomas die?"

The bearded farmer grunted. "Happened last fall."

He quickly did the calculations, then sighed. His father had probably received the news of his presumed death after the prison break. That would shock any father's heart.

His own chest squeezed in sympathy.

If only their reunion had not been stolen by such incomplete news. But at least they had exchanged enough letters over the years to assure him that his father was not completely disappointed in Nicholas anymore.

He spooned a few more bites of stew as he struggled to maintain his composure and sorted out the ramifications.

His father was not waiting at the castle, which meant there would be no joyous reunion. But there was still a home waiting for him. Safe walls within which to heal and grieve as he assumed the role of baronet.

Wait. The steward had spoken of a current baronet in that position.

It must be a distant relative who had assumed the title with Nicholas presumed dead on the continent.

Someone who might not appreciate his resurrection.

Nicholas needed to be prepared before he showed up on the man's doorstep.

He reached out to tug on the farmer's sleeve. "Who lives at Muncaster now?"

The man rose and began to move away as if to avoid more conversation, then tossed his reply over his shoulder. "Sir Nicholas and his bride."

Nicholas' breath caught in his lungs and he almost choked on his tongue.

Someone—somehow—was impersonating him to the point that the townspeople believed the ruse.

Who looked enough like him—?

Heat rushed through his veins until he was lightheaded.

There was one man.

And the last time Nicholas had seen him, the scoundrel was wearing Nicholas' officer's coat and they were both on their way to a lifetime as slaves.

He must have gotten himself ransomed by impersonating Nicholas.

He pushed away the remnants of his meal, thoroughly sickened by the betrayal of a supposed friend.

And then the rest of the farmer's revelation finally sank in.

The impostor had taken a bride.

Any bride or Nicholas' bride?

He recalled all those nights when he'd told his crew about the castle and the few when he'd spoken of a bride to come home to.

If the knave were bold enough to steal a title, he would certainly have tried to steal a wife as well.

But if that were true, how could his Susannah have married another? Not when his memories of the girl and her song had kept him sane all those years. Why couldn't she have remained faithful to him...and not yield to one claiming his name?

A simple meal in a pub should not have upended his world in such a manner...and yet it was better to have discovered the shocking news before reaching Muncaster's doorstep.

To have lost his father, name, home, and betrothed in a single blow was more than he could comprehend and his hands shook with barely contained rage.

Justice had to be done before he was fully avenged and the Pennington name restored. And like war, he needed to infiltrate the enemy's camp to get information.

For now, he would keep his beard and humble clothing as a disguise.

Nicholas eyed the steward busy talking with the other townsfolk across the room and knew God had given him an opportunity.

* * *

After paying for his meal, Nicholas lingered in the pub awaiting his chance to speak with the steward.

His first goal was to seek employment...in his own castle.

He cracked his knuckles, but now was not the time for anger. Seeking calm, he recalled the kind of garden he had once imagined while overseas.

A terrace overlooking the valley. With rhododendrons.

His traitorous mind inserted the image of a girlish face beside a cliff and he ground his teeth together at the memories.

Across the room, the steward rose and prepared to leave.

With a nod of thanks to the proprietor, Nicholas exited first. Then loitered outside as if studying the nearby sea.

The man emerged and quickly started down the road leading to Muncaster.

"Excuse me, Mr. Ellis."

The steward turned, then eyed Nicholas' attire and bearing.

Too late, Nicholas realized he should act like a humble laborer but his heritage and years as a military officer had lent strength to his spine. He deliberately slouched his posture. "I overheard inside that you are hiring a gardener."

Mr. Ellis raised an eyebrow as he focused on Nicholas' face.

He looked away from the man's penetrating gaze. "Of late I have been away to sea, but I have always loved the out of doors." He waved a hand toward the valley opening up to the ocean. "And I should think this God-given natural beauty would serve as ample inspiration for a household garden."

"Have you any experience gardening?"

Nicholas caught his breath. Why had he not thought of his qualifications? "No. But I always wished to and I am not afraid of hard work."

"Where did you say you were from?"

"I had not said." He scrambled for more of the truth. "I have spent the last decade in various places along the Atlantic, mostly at sea, but my childhood was spent in a valley not unlike this one." He endured another assessing look.

"And your name?"

His eyes widened. He had truly not thought out the ruse for he could not use his own name or a variation, but needed to be called something.

Just promise you'll make the most of the remainder of your life."

Nicholas swallowed hard. "I go by Stefan."

God, please forgive me for my lies and if he still lives, be with my friend wherever he is.

The steward nodded slowly. "Very well, *Stefan*. You will do for a trial." He eyed Nicholas' tattered clothing again, then reached into his purse for a few coins. "This is only an advance against your wages so you can acquire decent shoes and garments."

Nicholas endured a wave of shame...and gratitude. "Thank you, sir."

Mr. Ellis offered a small smile. "The position includes a room above the stables and meals with the household staff. Once you are presentable, make haste to Muncaster. The stablemaster will show you where to leave your belongings, then come find me so we can go over the particulars."

Nicholas nodded for his throat was swollen with emotion.

The steward gave him another speculative look, then with a shake of his head, turned toward Muncaster and continued on his way.

Nicholas blew out a breath.

After being hired with room and board, he would not have to worry about his next meal or where he would lay his head that night.

Thank the Almighty for small blessings.

Then again, he would be at Muncaster where he should be inside the stone walls rather than above the stable.

No. He had always preferred the rustic.

What was with his conflicted emotions today?

He fingered the coins in his hand, then turned to study the nearby establishments. A general store for clothing...and then two doors down was a rooming house run by Mrs. Haddington. He smiled. The widow used to have a softness for vagabonds and would probably offer a bath.

An hour later, Nicholas neared the stableyard clean and with two additional sets of new clothes in his knapsack. He still wore his thick beard as a disguise as well as to aid his adjustment to the colder climate after all those years nearer the Equator.

But this close to home, the flood of memories left him both homesick and overwhelmed by joy.

Thank You God for sparing my life. Now help me set things to right.

Anger flashed, followed by guilt. Would God really bless plans of revenge? Perhaps he should seek justice instead for there had to be an adequate penalty for impersonating a titled man in order to claim his inheritance.

But one could not reverse a marriage and restore a woman to her rightful groom...

Bitterness swirled in his gut.

His musings were interrupted as a man exited the stables. "Are you Stefan?"

He nodded, then as he continued his approach, he realized the man was a larger version of his boyhood friend Harold.

"Mr. Ellis said to expect the new gardener." Harold stared as if highly curious.

Nicholas averted his eyes to avoid the moment of recognition, but that action only drew his attention to the different horses in the various stalls...and a dog that was likely a descendant of the original pair.

A smile curved his lips before he could stop it.

"Well, *Stefan*..." Harold coughed.

Nicholas' eyes darted to those of his frowning friend whose eyes are filled with confusion and a bit of pain.

"I'm sure you have your reasons for taking such employment." Harold cleared his throat. "You can take my father's old room for the time being."

"His old room?" Did that mean? "Harold, my condolences—"

The man offered a sad smile. "And I to you."

Tears stung his eyes. Had it only been a few short hours since learning of his father's passing?

Nicholas could only manage a nod in response.

Harold glanced toward the main castle and squared his shoulders. "For as long as the *garden* takes, you will find the proper tools in the shed at the corner."

He knew exactly where that was.

"And in the meantime, there are many a mount needing exercise should you find yourself with free time to assist."

Nicholas clapped a hand on Harold's shoulder. "'Tis good to know I have a friend here in the stableyard." He glanced at the castle himself. "However, after all these years, who among those walls is likely to see through my temporary alias?"

His friend pursed his lips. "The cook is the same and perhaps a few of the lower maids but I doubt they saw you often enough to have a strong memory."

Except Nicholas could recall many a motherly moment from the cook.

Harold shrugged. "Sir Thomas replaced the steward about three years ago and you have already passed his scrutiny. The new, er, baronet immediately replaced the butler, housekeeper, and your father's valet."

"So, I have only the promised meals to worry about until I can contrive a way to see Mrs. Jennings alone to win her cooperation."

His friend hummed. "I'll see what I can do about her packing a basket for the time being...since I'm sure the new gardener will have much to do attuning himself to the grounds."

He offered another nod of thanks, then squared his shoulders. "I was to find Mr. Ellis when I arrived."

"Then we'll talk later, *Stefan*." Harold winked. "Interesting choice of name."

Nicholas swallowed hard. "He was another friend in time of need."

A path without indenture papers or the vile threat of commitment.

God, grant me the courage to face this unwelcome fate.

~February 1814

Susannah busied herself in the corner of the castle kitchen, stirring a batch of tea cake batter as other servants bustled in and out.

Over the past month, she had settled into the household routines. Most of the regular staff had forgotten about her indenture, and while her duties were still centered around the familiarity of the kitchen, she had been accepted into their ranks. And until now, she had almost been able to pretend that her time here was part of that once-conceived plan to find employment outside of Liverpool.

She dropped spoonfuls of batter onto a baking sheet and slid it into the brick oven.

However, today the staff was in an uproar of anticipation and dread for the Penningtons were finally returning to Muncaster after an extended stay in Bath.

Meaning that she was now stuck under the same roof as multiple daily reminders of their betrayal.

God, give me strength.

A few minutes later, there was an increase in activity and the sound of many footsteps and slamming doors. But down in the kitchen, Susannah focused on transferring the fresh tea cakes to a cooling rack.

Anything to keep her mind occupied and her tears at bay.

Before long, her roommate arrived with orders from the butler for two tea trays. "One for the master in his study, and the other for the mistress in her rooms." Edith lowered her voice. "While I

He pivoted quickly before the emotions spilled over, then jogged to the stairs and stowed his belongings in the elder Mr. Baxter's room...escaping in a rush before more memories and losses overtook him.

Minutes later, Nicholas approached the front door.

Too late, he realized he should have used the servants' entrance but the door was already opening and a stern-looking man in livery admitted him.

At least this member of the staff wasn't giving him suspicious looks.

But then again, any newly hired staff members would never question the identity of the baronet and would naturally take the impostor's side against Nicholas' claims. He would need to think through his strategy.

"I am here to see Mr. Ellis."

The servant sniffed and lifted his chin. "I am Mr. Morton. Our steward said to expect you but I am quite convinced he will acquaint you with the proper entrance for the lower staff should you ever need entrance to the castle again." The butler turned and led the way down a familiar corridor and past the closed door of his father's study.

In addition to the echo of memories, he could hear noise inside.

Fresh anger had him clenching his fists, but it was not the time for the confrontation seeing the man's face would bring.

However, an itchy feeling crawled over his skin to be back within these walls at the same time as such evil.

He had to get away...

Nicholas quickly caught up to the butler who had stopped outside the door to his mother's private parlor. After knocking, Nicholas was shown into a room that had been transformed into an office.

The old steward's office had been housed above the carriage house, but it made sense for the steward to be closer to the household operations.

Mr. Ellis looked up from a stack of papers and his eyes swept over Nicholas' cleaned-up attire. A strange look passed over his face before it was schooled into a businesslike expression. "Are you settled in at the stables?"

"I am. And I am eager to explore the gardens. To see what needs to be done, of course." Nicholas stuck his hands into his pockets, trying to contain the urge to bolt.

However, unlike his childhood, there were no tutors or lessons to avoid. Only an impostor who would not easily give up his ill-gotten gains.

Mr. Ellis rose and stepped around the end of his desk. "Yes. Before you begin your duties, I must introduce you to Lady Pennington for it was her idea to improve the grounds and she may have specific ideas in mind." He moved to the door.

Lady Pennington.

Nicholas caught his breath but he could not protest now...

The harsh reality of his losses was piling onto his shoulders but he reluctantly followed the steward abovestairs.

Surprisingly, the man stopped not at his parents' old suite of rooms, but at the sitting room attached to his own childhood quarters.

The room where many of his lessons had taken place.

After a quick knock, an imperious voice called out from within. "Enter."

Mr. Ellis opened the door. "Lady Pennington, as requested, I have secured the services of a gardener." The steward waved him forward.

Nicholas braced himself for the encounter, then stepped through the doorway.

Through respectfully down-turned eyes, he observed a some-what nondescript brown-haired woman in a pale blue gown seated before the fire with an overly ornate shawl draped about her shoulders and an embroidery hoop in her hands.

She turned to her left just enough to sweep critical eyes over his simple attire, eventually wrinkling her nose presumably at the beard on his face.

Nothing about her felt familiar, but from his position near the door, he could not see enough of her arm to note if there was a scar there. And it would be unseemly for him to ask her for a song...

But if this shell of a woman was indeed the adventurous girl of his youth, either life—or marriage to his impostor—had stolen much, for she little resembled the vision who haunted his dreams.

"You'll do." She turned back to her needlework.

Mr. Ellis frowned slightly. "Did you have any specific instructions for the gardens?"

The woman huffed. "I care not. Only that it be impressive enough to attract the admiration of visitors. If my husband will not venture to London, I must bring society here."

Since when did a barefoot Cumbria lass with a love of waterfalls desire the crowded streets of a big city?

"You are dismissed." A wave of her lily-white hand compelled them out of the room and Nicholas was the first to escape with more questions than answers.

In the hall, the steward cleared his throat. "Very well. You have your task before you." He led Nicholas back toward the main floor and his office. "Once you have assessed the grounds and formulated a plan, send word and I will approve any necessary expenditures."

Send word? He sighed with relief that he would not be required to enter these walls for regular reports.

"Of course." He nodded as a subservient should. "I will see myself out and begin my work."

He avoided the nosy butler and those he might encounter in the kitchens as he darted for freedom, his mind already overflowing with possibilities.

He was home again in his beloved Eskdale Valley with the freedom to ignore business pursuits for the time being and instead create his dream garden.

Even if there were lilies and rhododendrons in it to honor the dream girl who turned out to be a nightmare...

Chapter Eleven

"**I** saw the most interesting stranger yesterday in town."

As the upstairs maid regaled the kitchen staff with a detailed report of her outing on her day off, Susannah continued peeling root vegetables.

They were nearing the bottom of the barrel of last year's crop, but Mrs. Jennings said they should soon have fresh vegetables arriving by sea to tide them over until their gardens began producing.

In Liverpool, she had seen an unusual glass structure that permitted growth year-round. Perhaps she could suggest such a thing to the cook later for the betterment of the castle at large.

"He was a bit rough around the edges from his apparent travels..." Dinah giggled. "...but so deliciously tall that I just know he would look dashing in a proper suit."

Edith sighed and Susannah bit back a smile. Dinah seemed to be a notorious flirt who was well acquainted with all the region's single men. And therefore, logically the first to notice a newcomer.

Mrs. Jennings scolded them to keep their focus on their work, but she wore a small smile as if remembering her own youthful infatuations. Something it appeared they all had in common.

Not that she could ever tell the others of her own childhood crush.

God, wherever the real Nicholas is, protect him and bring him home.

Dinah shifted the conversation toward other things, then after a bit retreated back to her duties.

Susannah glanced about the overly warm room at the remaining staff. Once there were no more summons to Susan's side, she had slowly regained their trust.

It had probably helped matters that she had confided in both Mrs. Jennings and her roommate enough to say that she and Susan had a difficult *history* and that Susannah suspected she was sent to Muncaster as a punishment.

Additional sympathy grew once the women acquired their own opinions regarding the lady of the house after several meal complaints and eavesdropping on Mrs. Finch's frustrations during a haphazard redecorating attempt.

With her peeling complete, Susannah gathered the scraps and deposited them into the waste bucket sitting beside an overflowing twin. She turned to the cook. "Mrs. Jennings? Should I carry these out to the rubbish pile?" She would welcome the excuse to be out-of-doors for even a minute.

The woman grimaced as she removed fresh loaves of bread from the oven, releasing another wave of heat into the room. "I had forgotten. Harold relayed a message earlier that there is a new gardener. A...Stefan?...who requested we save the vegetable scraps for him in order to enrich the soil somehow."

"What a novel idea." She raised her eyebrows.

"Perhaps." The woman shrugged. "Deliver the scraps to the gardener wherever he might be and ask where he wants them deposited in the future."

"Yes, ma'am." Choosing to forgo a shawl because she was already overheated, she gathered the buckets and turned for the door.

"Oh, and make sure he knows he is welcome to join us for our luncheon later..."

"I will." Moments later, she had exited the castle and took a deep breath of the fresh air. It was a beautiful day and even in the empty kitchen garden, there were glimpses of green as spring lay around the corner.

Soon someone—perhaps the very gardener she was to find—would need to prepare the vegetable beds, but at least for today, his duties were elsewhere. She thought of the vast lawns on the western side of the castle, but before exploring that direction, she heard the murmur of voices to the east where there were more trees...and a view of the valley.

If she could not travel up the valley to Boot, she could at least enjoy the feeling of being close...

She adjusted her grip on the handles. It was truly unfortunate that she might have to circle the castle in order to explore all the possible locations where the new gardener might be...

With a growing smile, she turned toward the voices. She had truly missed the jaunts of her childhood and could pretend today's duty was one of them.

As she walked around the end of the castle, she began to hum the melody of a hymn. Off ahead to her left and past the stableyard was the church where she had fully embraced the truth that even as an unwilling servant, she was still a child of God.

She was seen by the Almighty and that was enough.

Off in the distance with the picturesque valley beyond them, she spied the stablemaster bidding farewell to another man, then disappearing through the trees on his way toward his usual domain.

The remaining man picked up a shovel and began digging another in a straight line of holes.

It seemed she had found the gardener.

She detoured that direction, finally putting words to her song. Based on the man's height and wide shoulders, he might be the same person Dinah had been gossiping about.

As she neared, the gardener looked up, staring at her as he brushed brown hair off his forehead with the back of his hand. She thought that a smile flitted about his lips but it was hard to see beneath his thick beard.

Something about him seemed familiar and her voice faded into silence.

His dark eyes scanned her attire and landed on the buckets she carried. His shoulders slumped. "You've brought the scraps I asked for." He dropped the shovel.

Curiosity got the better of her and she nodded toward the holes. "What new feature will these be?"

"I envisioned a long terrace bordered by a hedge of alternating yew pillars and box to give shelter from the wind while yet keeping a view of this beautiful valley." He turned as if to admire the scenery.

In her mind's eye, she saw the possibilities and she lowered the heavy pails to the ground. "It would make for a lovely place to take a walk. Or for children to play." Her voice trailed off for they would not be her children.

The man cleared his throat. "I thought to relocate rhododendron from further up the valley to this location where they would be sheltered but still bring beauty."

Her heart pounded harder. Rhododendron flourished around her waterfall and the thought of having those precious memories close at hand to admire misted her eyes with emotions. She had not ventured there since finding her father's body.

"I might also order lilies and other flowers to intersperse among the trees."

Lily.

Her father's pet name in the valley where he died.

It was her turn to clear her throat as she wrapped her arms around her midsection. "You have certainly taken on a large task."

"Someone once told me I could do anything if I put my mind to it." A wistful tone colored his voice.

Something about his words nagged at her memories, but then he turned away from the valley and his eyes widened as he stepped closer. "Forgive my poor manners."

He had been yammering on about plants when the poor maid had only been sent to deliver the kitchen scraps.

The woman scurried backward at his quick approach, then stopped when he picked up the buckets she'd abandoned.

Her crossed arms fell to her sides. "It appears I forgot my task as well." She glanced back toward the castle as if measuring the distance. "The pails were overflowing but the cook did not know where you wished them deposited."

"Come." He grasped the handles and cut through a wooded section toward the stables. A moment later, he heard the sound of swishing skirts behind him and the tread of shoes on the path underfoot.

But otherwise, silence.

Unlike the sweet melody he'd heard earlier that had sent his heart soaring.

And then he'd turned from his labor to catch a glimpse of a beautiful woman with glorious auburn hair...and a servant's garb.

Fool.

As a knight—baronet—of the realm, he had no business being attracted to a servant. The country was littered with fatherless children due to such dalliances. Not to mention that—until yesterday—he had believed himself engaged.

To the haughty shell of a woman who was now married to another.

While he might be free to choose his own bride now, she must not be one from among the lower classes. Something his father would have insisted upon were he still alive.

Nicholas' chest ached with the memory of visiting the chapel graveyard last evening. Standing between the graves of his parents, he had vowed to restore the Pennington name and could not disgrace it now.

As he emerged from the shadow of the trees into the clearing behind the stables, he shook off the melancholy mood, then paused until the maid joined him before starting forward again.

"I have started a compost pile in the corner near the tool shed." He transferred the buckets to one hand and pointed with the other. "I will see about placing a covered barrel in the kitchen gardens to make it more convenient in the future."

He emptied the pails of their contents and turned to the woman...who was staring at his shoulders. And arms.

A flicker of heat burned in his chest but he quickly squelched his attraction. Baronets did not court maids.

"Here." With a sharp tone, he thrust the buckets her direction.

She blinked as if in a fog, then a pretty blush rose on her cheeks as she reached out to grasp the handles. Allowing him to see the long jagged line on the inside of her left arm.

He suddenly recalled binding a similar injury on a much smaller arm.

His voice was rough as he spoke much harsher than he intended. "Where did you get that scar?"

The flash of fear in her green eyes at his tone was quickly replaced with a bit of fire. "Where, as in the cause, which was an injury? Or where, as in the location of the unhappy accident where I fell down a cliff?" She snatched the buckets and took a step back. "Not that my condition is any of your business."

He stared into the green eyes of a woman who was not born to be a maid but rather his wife. "What is your name?" He advanced on her.

Another flash of fear stopped him in his tracks. "They call me Anna."

Susannah. Anna.

There was more to the change than a simple nickname.

How had John come to marry the wrong girl?

His anger over the betrayal faded slightly knowing that his Susannah was beyond the man's clutches.

His eyes swept over her again, adjusting his mental image of the child by the waterfall to the changes maturity had brought. His blood heated to know it was perfectly acceptable to be attracted to his betrothed.

But she noticed the change in his attentions and was retreating cautiously.

As if he was judging her...or about to make an untoward claim with unwelcome attentions.

She lifted her chin but a weak voice emerged. "Mrs. Jennings also wanted me to convey that you are welcome to join the staff luncheon at one o'clock."

Mrs. Jennings, the dear cook and his surrogate mother. It was too soon when he was so unsettled. The woman would see right through him before he was prepared.

He shook his head.

"Suit yourself." Susannah turned on her heel and sped along the path toward the castle, the empty buckets swinging at her sides and the sun glinting on the red tones in her brown hair.

She was just as beautiful as he'd envisioned.
Dear God, bring justice. For both of us.

Susannah hurried back to the castle, chased by visions of the man's size. And the deep dark eyes that touched her soul and caused all sorts of fluttery feelings around her heart.

For a moment she had hoped he was Nicholas...but why return as a gardener and call himself Stefan? No, the boy she knew would...

Well, he would kill a fox and climb down a cliff to rescue a girl, but would he truly allow another man to steal his identity simply so he could remain out of doors with a view of the valley?

Then again, back on that eventful day, she seemed to recall Nicholas speaking with general distaste for his tutors and the heavy weight of his father's expectations.

That boy might pull a temporary ruse to escape his lessons...but the same boy had later been commended for his war actions, honored with a Pennington title, and became an officer in the Royal Navy.

Such a warrior would not deny his heritage. Would he?

Back inside the kitchen, she returned the pails to their corner and explained to Mrs. Jennings about the pile behind the stables and a soon to arrive barrel just outside in the garden.

The cook nodded. "Is the gardener coming to lunch?"

"Not today." Susannah retreated to the sink to wash dishes, glad for the time alone to get her thoughts and emotions back in order after such an unsettling encounter.

However, the new gardener might as well have attended their brief luncheon for he was the topic of conversation.

Harold had directed a strange look at Mrs. Jennings. "Our new gardener settled into his quarters as if he'd been there before and knew right where the tools were. He is quite comfortable out of doors. I even saw him tie a few knots like he'd been at sea..."

Mrs. Jennings looked thoughtful for a moment and then her shoulders relaxed with something that resembled relief as a slight smile played about her lips. But when she opened her mouth as if to respond, Harold gave a quick shake of his head and brushed a finger across his lips as if warning her to silence.

Susannah's heart pounded. Was it possible that her earlier suspicions were true?

She was not the only one around the table to detect the hint of a secret and a flurry of comments erupted as several recalled the gaunt man with thick head bandages who had arrived months before and then sequestered himself after replacing the loyal servants who had been closest to Nicholas as a child.

Now that the same man was physically recovered and fattened on sweets and spirits, he still did not venture out of his study unless he was away on business. But in those few glimpses, he did not resemble his father or the portraits of his supposed mother.

A heavy silence descended on the room, until Edith finally blurted out the question of the day. "Could there have been a switch?"

Susannah stared at her plate and bit her lip. It would never do to state she had spotted the impostor within minutes of meeting him.

However, others were beginning to understand the ramifications of a man falsely posing as another.

One of the footmen even questioned the convenient timing of the late baronet's demise in London, and Susannah joined several others in whispered prayers for justice.

"What can servants do to right such a wrong?" Edith twisted her napkin in her hands. "No one would believe our doubts."

Meanwhile Susannah's heart ached with the knowledge that she had been replaced too. But unlike Nicholas, no one else had cared.

The same footman leaned forward to look the others in the eyes. "How many of us knew the young master before he left home? Do we have any proof?"

Multiple pairs of eyes turned toward Mrs. Jennings. And Harold.

"Harold?" Edith frowned. "You grew up here in the stables..."

Susannah recalled the horse Nicholas had ridden. If anyone else was to recognize the boy-turned-man, it was he. But would he admit the truth that he'd known it was Nicholas wielding the shovel to create a terrace?

Harold sighed, then nodded. "We bide our time in silence—" He made eye contact with all who were gathered, including Mrs. Jennings. "Complete silence to any outside this room until such a time as *he* reveals his intentions and then we offer our support."

A few grumbled and whispered about righting the wrongs but, eventually everyone nodded.

Susannah blinked away the prick of tears, glad to know Nicholas was alive and not so far away. And obviously healthy and uninjured based on the muscles she'd been ashamed to have been caught ogling earlier.

And how had she reacted? By giving him a false name and running away.

True, she had been flustered by his proximity and ever aware of her stepmother's threats should she reveal her identity. But would he think her actions a rejection?

Surely she would have opportunity to explain herself later?

Her stomach cramped and she pushed away her mostly-empty plate.

Unless he did not remember her at all.

Except why the pointed interest in her scar? The staring that grew warmer and caused so many tingles on her skin...

No, she had to investigate further.

She could not wait for him to reveal his intentions as Harold insisted. She needed to know if the switched identity was intentional or an injustice to be corrected.

If her faith in him all these years had been misplaced.

Chapter Twelve

D ays passed without an opportunity for Susannah to talk to Nicholas.

He avoided meals with the rest of the staff and instead, Cook sent baskets of food to the stables with Harold.

Beyond the new waste barrel in the kitchen garden, she had no logical or reputation-preserving reason to venture out of doors. Not to mention, her allotted leisure time was still days away.

A growing desperation to explain herself led to a loss of appetite and restless nights. Something had to change or else she might do something foolish.

Mrs. Jennings found her pounding out her frustrations on the butter churn and frowned. "I know not what transpired the day you took the scraps to...the new gardener, but he is requesting you by name to be re-assigned."

Nicholas had asked for her by name? That was either very good...or very bad. *Dear God, please don't let him send me back to Liverpool...*

Susannah eased her grip on the wooden paddle. "Re-assigned?"

The woman narrowed her eyes as if assessing her worth or trying to see through to her secrets. "To assist him with the kitchen gardens and other flower beds until further notice." She huffed. "Said he needed a woman's opinion."

Her heart raced at the possibility of spending time with Nicholas away from prying eyes.

Mrs. Jennings must have seen something in her expression for her frown increased. "Watch yourself and tread carefully."

"Because of Mrs. Finch?" She could not help but remember the housekeeper waving the indenture papers and declaring Susannah must start in the kitchens. She would not take kindly to having her decision set aside, especially by another presumed servant.

The cook shook her head. "She could be a problem, although I believe she has forgotten you are here."

True. She had not seen the upper staff in weeks.

Mrs. Jennings cleared her throat. "I speak of the gardener. You are privy to our knowledge of his identity. Do not think to advance yourself above your station with an untoward flirtation."

The resulting burst of anger at being so judged was tempered only by the knowledge that the woman did not know she was a knight's daughter. Or that she was betrothed to the man.

Susannah threw her shoulders back. "I know the position of my birth and will behave accordingly." Let the woman take that truth however she willed.

Mrs. Jennings crossed her arms. "I have watched over that boy since his mother died and I am not stopping now."

"You have nothing to fear from me in that regard." After all, that boy was her hero.

The woman appeared slightly appeased. "Finish processing the butter before you desert us." She started for the door, then paused. "Other than the location of your service, nothing else has changed."

Susannah nodded.

She still had a roof over her head and meals. A maid's dress on her back. Forged indenture papers in the hands of the impostor or his minions. And a stepmother's threats to send her to Bedlam.

But very soon she would see Nicholas again and learn his intentions.

Her smile grew.

She tried to recall what she could of his eyes above that distracting beard, but all she truly remembered from their recent encounter was his size and strength.

Just like when she had been plastered to his back as a child...

Her face felt aflame as she hurried to strain the buttermilk, fill the molds, and rinse the churn.

After finishing her tasks, she glanced out the high window to assess the weather, then detoured to her shared room for her cloak and a pair of gloves to protect her hands.

Once outside, she spied Nicholas with a rake clearing away the old growth and fallen leaves in the kitchen gardens. With a quick glance to assure herself they were alone, she headed his direction.

After all, she needed to receive her instructions and no one should fault her for speaking with the gardener even if she must keep a proper distance...

However, her rehearsed words for their next encounter evaporated the closer she got and butterflies swarmed in her midsection.

"Come now, Susannah, I do not bite." He glanced over his shoulder at her with a smile that eased her worries. Especially since he called her by name.

"Nor do you allow rabid foxes to bite either." Her eyes misted at the memories. "Welcome home, Nicholas. Forgive me for not recognizing you earlier."

He glanced down at his clothes. "What gave it away?"

"Aside from the fact you just called me Susannah?" She raised an eyebrow, then relented with a full confession. "I suspected based on your eyes, your talk of the valley, and your size. Then those inside confirmed it with veiled references."

His eyes widened with panic. "What did they say?"

"A lot of speculation, but generally a decision to bide their time awaiting your direction and a promise not to speak of you to the new butler or housekeeper." He relaxed at her words, but she had to know. "Why?"

"Why what?"

"Why the ruse? What happened to cause another to take your rightful place and you sneak home? Were you that anxious to remain out of doors—"

"Never that." He slashed the air with his hand and fire lit his eyes. "I am a Pennington and know my duty." He eyed the castle with longing. "Thoughts of home kept me sane."

She shook her head. "Then why...?" She gestured weakly at his current attire and the garden implement in his hand.

"I needed more information." He sighed, then led her to a near-by bench where it could appear to anyone observing that they were discussing the gardens.

Once seated, he glanced at the castle again and sneered. "Tell me what you know of my supposed return."

"In September, your father sent word that you had been captured by pirates and a ransom was being arranged."

Nicholas whipped his gaze from the castle to her. "He knew that much? He did not think I was killed in battle in the Pyrenees mountains or during the prison break afterward?"

She gasped. "You were in a prison? On land and not at sea? I thought you were—"

"I was in the Royal Navy. However, our ship cannons were sometimes loaned to come to Wellington's aid on land. But after covering the army's retreat from one battle and being captured by the French, I helped our men to escape only to find myself injured and days later in the hands of barbarians."

Despite the fact he sat safely by her side, her heart pounded with fear for his well-being while her mind flooded with a multitude of questions. "So... But..."

He waved aside her stumbling attempts and pierced her with a steady gaze. "Tell me more of this ransom."

She blinked. "Your father was journeying to London to meet with the mediator and was eager to be reunited." What else had the letter said?

"Eager?" She caught a glimpse of the boy yearning for his father's approval.

"Very. He wrote of his pride at the man you had become. I saved the letter if you wish to read it for yourself."

He swallowed hard. "And then what happened?"

"A few weeks later we received word from the steward that there had been a reunion and a subsequent altercation with thieves on the docks. Your father was fatally wounded and you—er, someone—was returning here to recuperate from his injuries and mourn."

He frowned. "What does this someone look like?"

"I only encountered him once back in February." She looked to the castle, then shivered at the memory of the man's quick temper and how her scar repulsed him. "He is tall like you. Brown hair. Amber colored eyes that are simply cold and unfeeling. I knew immediately that he was not you."

"Then how did the other staff not recognize him last fall and do something?" He clenched a fist on his knee.

The visible evidence of his simmering emotions roused worries that he might be as violent as the impostor and she weighed her words before responding. "I was not here then, but a few days ago, the others mentioned a multitude of bandages on a gaunt man. And the immediate replacement of key household personnel. Other than a few trips on business, he has been isolating himself in the study or abovestairs."

Nicholas stared at his boot-clad feet as he processed what she had said.

Meanwhile, she reveled in examining the changes time had brought and tried to imagine his face without the current beard. There was no denying her flutter of attraction...

But another thought stunned her. When Nicholas was revealed as the true baronet, would he be married to her step-sister as if by proxy? Fear gripped her heart to think she could lose him again.

She suddenly wished to hide him away.

Then was drowned in guilt for such a selfish thought.

He was a nobleman who deserved to be inside his castle instead of sleeping above the stables while another rested in luxury.

Which allowed one question to break the silence. "Who is the man inside?"

Nicholas' fists clenched again. "I suspect he is John, one of my crew members who happened to be wearing my officer's coat when we were captured by the pirates."

"Officer? But how...?" Once again the questions swirling in her mind could not come out in any comprehensible order.

He continued as if had not heard her. "We were separated onboard the pirate's ship and once we reached land, I never saw him again.

"But why would he pretend to be you...?"

A brittle laugh burst from his lips. "I suspect we would have to ask *him* to know the reason why, but John was never one to waste an opportunity especially if he believed me to be dead or forever enslaved."

She sucked in a quick breath.

Oh, how close she had come to losing him forever.

Nicholas took a deep breath and tried to relax his clenched fists as he processed all that Susannah had said.

His father had known he was alive and was eager for a reunion.

At some level, he'd known that last part to be true based on the veiled sentiment in the few letters he had received over the years. And yet, he would have given anything to see his face again.

If it truly was John inside—and he could imagine no other—reuniting with the elder baronet was just one more thing John had stolen.

A gnawing sense of suspicion edged into his thoughts.

If John was willing to use Nicholas' coat to impersonate an officer in order to be ransomed, how far would he go to avoid discovery once back in England? Or had he simply been lucky and took advantage of yet another opportunity after the thieves attacked?

Bitter rage clawed at his stomach.

"What are you going to do about it?" Susannah's soft voice startled him for a moment. "You cannot keep pretending to be a gardener."

Irritation sparked. "*You* cannot keep pretending to be a maid."

She winced and fear flashed in her eyes. "It was not my choice."

A surge of protectiveness welled up. "What happened? Because I do not believe your father would have allowed—"

Her face contorted. "If only he were alive..."

He reached for her gloved hand and squeezed it in sympathy.

She drew in a quick breath but did not pull away.

Society might frown upon their unchaperoned contact, but he and Susannah had survived a more compromising position together in the past as he carried her up the cliff.

"Tell me," he whispered. "What has happened in your life while I was at war?"

She stared at the barren vegetable beds spread before them. "About a year after your father's promotion to baronet and our...uh, their...agreement..."

He squeezed her hand tighter and smiled. "If you recall, I accepted our betrothal."

A hint of pink colored her cheeks as she darted a glance his direction, then away. "And I."

While their arrangement wasn't traditional in any way given their decade of separation, he would like to think that if he had not been impressed at sea, he would have courted her properly when she came of an age.

Their fathers had secured their future, but now it was up to him to get to know the woman she had become.

She sighed. "In hopes to give me a woman's influence, my father married a widow from Carlile who brought two daughters my age. Susan and Prudence."

"A Susan and Susannah under one roof?" His eyebrows rose.

"Exactly." She sighed again. "Which is why when my father died a year later and we were forced by the heir to move to Liverpool, my stepmother began calling me Anna. I lost my father, my home, and my name, but I still had the possibility of you. Until she stole that too."

He rubbed a thumb over the back of her hand. "How?"

"When they first married, my father begged me to do all I could to get along with the new members of our family and ease their transition to country life. I suppose I set a bad precedent by always letting them get their way in matters that I did not care about." She shrugged. "I still had the falls, my valley, my father's love, and someday your return to look forward to." She risked another quick glance his direction.

His smile grew. "I looked forward to my return as well."

She bit her lip, then removed her hand only to twist her fingers together on her lap. "Yes, well, after settling in Liverpool, I grieved the loss of my father more deeply than the rest of the household who had known him a shorter time. So, while they entered the social circle, I was content to stay at home and eager to keep my hands busy."

"Leaving less time to think?" He had done the same in the past.

She nodded. "Over the years, I gradually descended into the role of a servant. However, when it came time for debuts and balls, I realized that my stepmother had no knowledge of our betrothal."

"How is that possible?" He frowned.

She lifted a delicate shoulder. "In the short duration of their marriage, I assume my father had not told her because there had been no need. You were gone from the region and I was but barely fifteen when he died."

"I can see how other matters would naturally take precedence, but why not on his deathbed?"

Her throat spasmed as she swallowed. "He died quite unexpectedly in the middle of a storm." She swiped a few tears from her cheek and drew a shaky breath. "It was the anniversary of his wedding to my mother and I found his body on the path to the waterfall."

The very waterfall that had been her mother's favorite spot and the place where a young girl had gone to mourn alone.

He reclaimed her hand and the silence stretched.

Once she seemed to have regained control of her emotions, he pressed forward with the original direction of the conversation. "If your father never told her about me, I assume you did not either."

She shook her head. "You were a precious memory that belonged only to me and thoughts of you were all I had left. Well, that and a ragged remnant of fox fur from an old cloak's hood."

He smiled in understanding. While he had shared many things with his fellow crew members over the years, he had also kept a few details about young Susannah close to his heart.

She squared her shoulders. "When the time came, my stepmother's focus was on launching her daughters and she seemed not to care that I was content on the fringes as a wallflower. Until the day your father's letter arrived announcing your coming return and she discovered our..."

"Betrothal?" He chuckled. "You know you can say the word."

Another flush colored her cheeks, but this time she met his eyes for longer. "It had been so long since I had heard from you that I began to think it was a lovely dream. Even though I prayed often for your safe return." Finally, a smile emerged that reminded him of a younger version of herself calling him a hero.

A smile that stirred his blood and beckoned him to taste her lips.

A smile that faded.

"Once my stepmother knew of you, she began to scheme and with your father's death, the current situation became possible."

She waved her free hand toward the castle and his heart stuttered. Surely... "The woman I met my first day... That was your sister?"

She winced. "Stepsister. But yes."

"How...?"

"The short version of that tale is that I was ambushed and locked away in my room the day Sir Nicholas called on us seeking to be reunited with his betrothed. Before the visit was complete, my stepmother had not only arranged the wedding but had the happy couple visit the bishop thereby cutting off all chance of protest. Especially when I was threatened with Bedlam as a jealous girl who wished for her sister's life."

Righteous anger on her behalf was cut short as her breath hitched.

With a cracking voice, she continued. "But almost worse than having my only means of escaping that household stolen was the fact that you—he—did not notice the switch. As if I was the only one who bothered to remember that day at the waterfall..."

He pivoted on the bench to face her. "Trust me, I remembered. And there were times those memories were the only thing keeping me sane."

Their gazes connected and held until her face flushed and she looked down at her lap, plucking at her apron. "Despite her threats of having me locked away permanently, I held out a bit of hope when I was sent here before the wedding, but the bridegroom had already departed. And then forged indenture papers were delivered to the housekeeper as a wedding gift."

Indentured? Was there any justice left?

She shook her head as if dispelling the memories. "Being forced to work here of all places with the reminder of my stepmother's deception around every corner was...difficult. Until the couple returned from their honeymoon and I encountered the man abovestairs and saw evidence of bruises on her arms."

He flexed his jaw. No woman—even if she had willingly partaken in fraud—deserved to be treated so roughly.

"Like the story of Joseph, what man meant for evil, God used for good. For knowing my stepmother, even if I had protested his identity, *I* could be the one married to that scoundrel..." Her small smile was followed by a sigh. "I admit I still struggle at times with the idea of forgiveness. And until you arrived, I had found a measure of contentment in my plan to finish out my indenture and then look for a position elsewhere."

At least she was not a prisoner to her bitterness.

He cleared his throat. "I know firsthand about being trapped in slavery and admire your outlook. I had a friend in Morocco—the real Stefan—who shared those same thoughts with me. He sacrificed himself for my freedom."

Stefan.

Nicholas had done the same during time of war to save his fellow sailors, soldiers, and prisoners. He did not regret any of those decisions. Had Stefan felt the same?

His friend would have liked his Susannah. However, their shared stories picked at his conscience.

What good could possibly have come from his identity and home being stolen? Why couldn't it have been him who was ransomed and returned to England? Then he would have been the one to travel to Liverpool to meet the bride and...

He might have been duped by her stepmother into marrying the wrong girl while simply thinking the years had changed her.

And an impostor—like John—without the true shared memories would have stood less chance of unmasking the ruse.

He recalled their conversations while on the run from the French. Times when the man expressed a detailed interest in the castle and area as well as his desire for a position of some sort. Unless the man had done something drastic—like impersonate a nobleman—he might have trusted John as a friend and introduced him to business connections in the area where he could have likely embezzled...

However, by carrying out the current scheme, such activities were likely already in place and eroding the very relationships his father had built.

Nicholas had to figure out a way to observe the false baronet without being seen, just to confirm his suspicions before making plans to restore their true identities and bring justice.

"Promise you'll make the most of the remainder of your life."
I will, Stefan. I will.

Susannah suddenly yanked her hand from his, then stood and added distance between them. A second later, he heard the whistling and the crunch of footsteps on gravel.

Reminding him of their proximity and what he should be doing to preserve her reputation.

He stood and pointed to the garden, while raising his voice. "As I was saying, if you would help clear the dead growth from the beds into a few piles, then I can turn the earth and we can develop a plan for the planting."

He noticed Harold cutting across toward the kitchen, perhaps for luncheon. How long had they been talking?

Beside him, Susannah nodded even though she deserved a life of leisure, not of toil.

He gestured toward the abandoned rake. "You can use that for now or ask Harold to open the tool room for you. I have a few more holes to dig on the terrace but will be back to check on you later."

Susannah quickly reached for the garden implement, but her pink cheeks revealed their earlier proximity.

He strode away before doing something foolish like pull her into his arms.

Chapter Thirteen

Nicholas spread a scoop of mulch on the third of many such paths between the beds of new plants in the kitchen garden. It was one of Susannah's ideas in order to discourage unwelcome weeds while eliminating the mud on all their shoes.

After all, the spring rains could be both a blessing and a curse.

He glanced to the corner where she was planting lilies and bluebells near the bench—their bench—under a tree. Susannah had thought the additional plantings would make a nice retreat for the staff who were not allowed in the formal areas but also deserved tp enjoy the castle grounds.

Such generosity only added to his attraction.

He had noticed her potential as a child, but the woman she'd become had him fighting a constant smile. Especially when she started singing as she was now.

She loved the out-of-doors as much as he.

He scattered more mulch and thought of the new terrace. There was a natural beauty in the wild valley that appealed more than the sculpted mazes popular in London palaces and he was pleased at the transformation.

As well as the excuse to spend time with Susannah.

Between the terrace and the kitchen garden, over the past weeks they had spent countless hours in conversation as they worked side by side. Conversations that had laid open their past mistakes and regrets, but also revealed glimpses of hope for their future.

Her stories of life as a virtual servant in Liverpool in the shadow of her supposed family members were sad but her joy at being back home in their valley had him asking about those previous years with her father and the waterfall.

Ever since learning that was where the knight had died, he'd wanted to take her there again to reclaim other memories such as the day they met...so on a day when the residing couple were away on business and shopping in Carlile, he arranged a trip with a few other servants in order to harvest plants for the terrace. All so she could see the place again while they were properly chaperoned.

There had been a moment in her favorite spot overlooking the waterfall...

Others might have thought she was admiring the view, until she asked if there were any wildlife like foxes in the area. He could only laugh as they shared a smile.

Ever since, her countenance had been lighter and she sang even more while planting the rhododendron in their new places over-looking the valley.

He moved further along the path with more mulch.

Of course, during their days together, Susannah had wanted to know all about his life at sea and how he'd proved himself worthy of knighthood and elevated the Pennington name to his father's pride. He tried to avoid the hard memories of war and death but still gave her a feeling of the ocean and the different lands and cultures he had experienced during those years.

News had recently arrived in Ravenglass that Wellington had finally captured Paris and forced Napoleon into exile.

The war was over for all the soldiers, not just him.

All but the lingering nightmares. But they were fading, mostly because Susannah invaded his dreams.

Daily it grew more difficult to restrain himself from making romantic advances on her person, but equally strong was the knowledge the time was coming soon to enact his revenge.

For just yesterday, he had finally seen John from a distance. And the resulting surge of bitterness had soured his mood for hours. Susannah had frowned at his reaction, but her eyes said she understood even as she gave him space to sulk.

He did not deserve one such as she...

With a scrape of the shovel, he realized he had emptied the wheelbarrow once again.

Two more loads should finish the current task...and then he would need to find another project to distract him from the injustices.

Unless...

"It's nearly time."

He startled at Susannah's voice at his elbow. Surely she couldn't know all his thoughts? "Time for...?"

"The luncheon meal if you will finally favor us with your presence." A smile flitted about her rosy lips.

Someday soon he would not need to protect himself by avoiding the staff and not setting foot inside the castle.

Susannah glanced at the sky and then at the finished bench area. "While I sometimes wonder what life would have been like had I not been so agreeable to my stepmother's demands as a child, I am glad for the chance to transform this space."

"Once the flowers take root and spread, it will be a beautiful retreat." He brushed a bit of dirt from her cheek and tucked a wisp of hair behind her ear. "Just like you will be a beautiful Lady Pennington someday."

A furious blush colored her cheeks but she could not hide the answering spark in her eyes even if propriety demanded that she skirt the topic.

He chuckled. "My father would certainly have approved."

"Oh, he already did." Her smile grew as if she knew a secret.

He raised an eyebrow. "You mean the betrothal agreement after you sang?"

"That, but also his last letter." Her eyes widened. "I promised to show you and forgot."

"Later." Since they were out of sight of the household, he reached for her hand. "After these past weeks, if we were not already bound, I would be down on one knee asking for your hand in marriage."

She gasped and the fluttering vein in her neck showed her heart was likely racing as fast as his.

"Surely you know that thoughts of you carried me through our separation."

A slight laugh escaped her lips. "Thoughts of a bleeding ragamuffin wandering the countryside? I was never very ladylike."

"You were—are—where it matters most. And the fact you love the outdoors, makes you perfect for me." He captured her gaze, desperate to communicate his sincerity. "But what I remember most is a haunting voice paying tribute to a mother's love. Bravery and courage in the face of pain. How you called me your hero and made me want to live up to such a title. How you believed I could excel at anything I set my mind to."

"All of that in one meeting?" She drew in a shaky breath.

"Yes."

Her eyes delved in to his. "Well, I remember thinking the village girls were quite right to find you handsome. How sweet you were to crown me with flowers to cheer me up. How resourceful you were to bandage my wounds." Her blush returned. "How strong you were to climb up that cliff with me on your back and then how safe I felt being held in your arms all the way home."

Heat rose in his veins at the thought of her wrapped around him now.

"It is no wonder I still have remnants of that fox's fur as a reminder of the day I was jealous of the older village girls for I was too young to get your attention."

"You had my attention. In fact, right before he announced he was sending me to sea, I even told my father that you'd grow up to be the village darling with beaus lined up for miles." He stepped closer. "I did not tell him I wished to be one of them, but somehow he came to the same conclusion and orchestrated a match."

A smile curved her plump lips. "On my part, my father might have heard me speak of you more than a few times. If only he could have lived to see the man you've become."

Another memory surfaced. *I have your bravery to thank for my lily's life.* He welcomed the happy weight of that ongoing responsibility.

Nicholas lifted her left arm and ran his fingers over her scar. Others might frown at the disfigurement, but he saw it as the symbol of the past that bound their hearts.

He raised her hand to his lips and pressed a kiss atop her knuckles. "My Lily, I know not how, but I vow to honor their wishes and stand for truth."

Susannah's heart felt like it was pounding out her chest at the heat in his eyes and the delicious tingles running up her arm where he had kissed her hand and touched her scar.

And his words.

Oh. To be someone's precious lily again made her heart swell.

She drew in a shaky breath and feared she might swoon. She might not see the path or battles ahead, but knowing Nicholas wished to emerge at the end as her husband and this castle as her home was a resurrection of all her hopes.

The flood of emotion sent tears to her eyes.

Dear God, restore Nicholas to his title. Give me the courage to fight by his side.

A finger swiped across her cheek removing a spilled drop, then he cupped his hand on the side of her neck before slowly lowering his head.

Firm lips covered her own gently, and then with more pressure until she clung to his waistcoat. Blood rushed in her head, leaving her knees shaky, but oh, what a sensation to have her first kiss in the arms of the man she loved.

For yes, she had come to love him over the past weeks of working together in the gardens.

He broke the kiss and she moaned at the deprivation of his lips, even if the soft whiskers of his beard had tickled. He chuckled, then rested his forehead against hers as they caught their breath. "Soon, my love."

Feeling brave and beautiful...and loved, she smiled. "How soon, my lord?"

His chuckle grew and he lifted his head. "I see I shall have to keep my wits and my head around you."

"Then I shall endeavor to keep my hands to myself." She smoothed the wrinkles in his waistcoat before dropping her arms to her sides.

She could not believe she was the one saying such things, but he wasn't rejecting her. Rather there was a flare in his eyes that matched the fire in her veins as wordless promises were exchanged.

Her cheeks hurt from her wide smile as she stared up into his eyes.

"Anna!"

She whipped her head around at the harsh scolding voice and saw Mrs. Jennings storming down the mulch-strewn path toward them.

"I am sorry, my lord, but I warned her not to reach above her station." The woman reached them, then with a tight grip on Susannah's arm, yanked her to an appropriate distance from Nicholas, then began to pull her toward the castle. "I had wondered why he specifically requested your help in the gardens, but you must have played the strumpet that first day."

She winced at the cook's accusation and her tight grip. "I didn't—"

"And then to take advantage of our luncheon revelations all to advance yourself? For shame." Mrs. Jennings made a clucking noise. "At least you abandoned your role as spy and did not tattle to Lady Pennington. Or did you?"

"Never." She glanced back at a frowning Nicholas who had been rooted in place, but was quickly catching up. "I would never tell her anything."

"Mrs. Jennings, release her at once."

The woman stopped their retreat halfway to the door and spun to face Nicholas, waving a mother-like finger in his face. "And you should know better. You bring shame—"

"No. I honor the commitment of my heart to the woman of my dreams." His fierce frown silenced the cook's second attempt at an argument while simultaneously releasing Susannah from the woman's grasp.

Once free, he offered his arm like a true gentleman and she rested her hand on his sleeve. Who would have imagined their using proper manners while standing in a kitchen garden dressed as servants?

"I also honor the agreement of our fathers." He grinned down at her but his words were for the sputtering cook. "May I present my betrothed, the real Miss Susannah Stanley, daughter of the late Sir William Stanley."

Her heart swelled with love but also pride at being truly recognized for herself once again. She turned to the squinting, obviously-doubtful woman and felt a flash of fear at the first challenge. "You will have to take my word for it, but the woman abovestairs is my stepsister, Susan."

Mrs. Jennings huffed. "'Tis convenient to now change your name from Anna."

"I have always been Susannah even though my stepmother shortened my name to avoid confusion with her own daughter."

The woman narrowed her eyes. "A likely story that could easily favor the other sibling."

Exactly why her stepmother's threats of Bedlam held such a hold over her life.

"Except the real Susannah would know exactly how and where we met." Nicholas turned her arm to expose her scar. "And bear evidence of the day she fell down the cliff beside the waterfall and know that I carried her to safety on my back."

She grinned. "After saving me from the rabid fox whose fur is still among my belongings even now."

The cook's eyes darted from Susannah's arm back to her face and she grew pale. "Oh, dear heavens, it is true." She dropped into a quick curtsy. "Forgive my impertinence for I sought only to protect Sir Nicholas—"

"You are forgiven." Susannah reached to place her free hand on the woman's shoulder. "Loyalty to the Penningtons is nothing to be ashamed of." She glanced up at Nicholas and found approval in his eyes.

"I thank you." Mrs. Jennings offered another head bob and then her gaze warmed. "I had my suspicions the day you arrived, but why didn't you say anything?"

She shook her head. "After locking me away before the wedding, my stepmother had also threatened to have me sent to an asylum if I attempted to reveal the truth of the switch in brides. For as you say, it was one sister's word against the other. Not to mention, just minutes before our introduction, I had been shocked with the revelation of the forged indenture papers and the depths of my stepmother's vindictive reach. I did not know who to trust."

Nicholas squeezed her hand atop his arm. "You can trust Mrs. Jennings."

She nodded and peace settled around her shoulders.

She was not alone. First, God. Then Nicholas. And now she had another ally in the house.

"How could she do that?" Mrs. Jennings scowled. "I understand how you might be afraid to speak the truth, but how could that woman speak vows before God..." She shook her head. "I am tempted to give her a piece of my mind."

Susannah glanced up at the castle in the direction of the couple's rooms and sighed. "Her personal aspirations might have compelled her to cooperate with her mother's schemes, but I pity her now." She recalled the bruises and other household rumors of more violence. "She is married to an impostor whose character leaves much to be desired."

Nicholas coughed beside her. "That is putting it mildly, my dear." He chuckled. "Nevertheless, I have to now admit relief to know John walked into your home in Liverpool instead of me. While I certainly would have doubted the bride's identity after being gone for so many years, would I have had any proof to void the contract with you being locked away out of sight?"

She bit her lip. She had never thought of that possibility.

"God spared me." Nicholas' voice cracked. "Us. What man meant for evil, God used for good. And where would I have begun to look for my dear Susannah if God had not brought her here?"

Their gazes locked in heavy realization of that truth.

Mrs. Jennings intruded on the moment. "Well, now that you are home and reunited, what are you going to do about it?"

Firm conviction joined her earlier peace. "It's time, Nicholas."

"Yes." He cleared his throat. "Time for luncheon for the both of you. But it's also time to plan our attack." He turned to Mrs. Jennings. "Can you arrange to slip away for a meeting this afternoon? On the terrace? I'll make sure Harold is also there."

The natural authority in his voice and his regal bearing left her breathless.

It was time for Sir Nicholas to shed his disguise and reclaim his family's honorable name.

Chapter Fourteen

N icholas was already waiting when Susannah arrived at the terrace.

She resisted the temptation to fall into his arms for another kiss, but instead reached into the pocket of her apron for the square of folded parchment. "Mrs. Jennings said she would be along shortly, but before I forget again..."

She handed Sir Thomas' letter to his son, then retreated to a stone bench in order to give him a moment of privacy to read the words she had memorized long ago.

I cannot express how I long to see my dear Nicholas again. Every day that passes is filled with regret over sending him to sea, but I cannot contain my pride at the man he has become. I pray he has not been too changed by his experiences, but I have no doubt he is a true credit to the Pennington name.

His shoulders shook with suppressed emotion as he absorbed his father's approval. Based on their previous conversations, she knew that Nicholas needed that knowledge to find peace with his father's untimely death.

He turned with misty eyes. "May I keep this for now?"

Tears pricked her own eyes at the longing in his voice. "Of course."

"Thank you for saving this." He tucked the missive into a pocket, then squared his shoulders. "It's time to fight so we can give him the next generation of Penningtons he so wished to see."

Heat rushed into her face. She had forgotten Sir Thomas' desire to hear the pitter patter of little feet inside the castle.

Nicholas chuckled and joined her on the bench. "Soon, my love. Soon."

Her heart soared to be called such. "Your father was not the only one proud of you. Or the only one to love you." Her voice trailed off at the realization of her bold declaration. Was it too soon?

His eyes flared with a new emotion, then his gaze dipped to her lips as if he wished to devour her.

Her own lips parted in anticipation, however whistling announced Harold's arrival a moment before he stepped out of the trees escorting Mrs. Jennings. Nicholas retreated an appropriate distance and gestured for the cook to take his former spot on the bench while Harold dropped to the grass.

Chaperones were both welcome and necessary, for with their declarations of love, it was becoming harder to maintain her distance. Especially when in the guise of a servant without the strict social boundaries of the upper class.

Nicholas tucked his hands behind his back and began to pace before the growing shrubs with the wide valley beyond. "I am a man of action and tired of waiting. It is time to fight for not only myself but also for Susannah and our future. We want our fathers' legacies to be honored and not buried in deceit and greed."

"Your fathers?" Harold turned to her with a frown. "Susannah? I admit my confusion."

Another person she had to convince. She sighed. "Nicholas, perhaps we should focus on you alone for now because it will be difficult to prove my identity."

He shook his head. "You obviously bear the scar you acquired on the cliff."

"You and I both know about that day and the rabid fox, but others could say it was a convenient story that we—"

"A rabid fox, you say?" Harold turned to Nicholas. "I remember you coming home without a shirt and blood on your jacket then telling such a tale while mentioning Sir William's daughter."

Her relief at the corroborating story was quickly followed by discouragement. "And yet you are a servant who could have been paid to say whatever Nicholas wished."

Nicholas frowned. "Paid with what? For I have no access to funds at present."

She turned pleading eyes toward him. "I am simply presenting the argument from the other side." She waved a hand at the castle. "We already know he has put his own people in positions of support who would testify as to *his* identity. And apparently the local officials in Ravenglass and your father's business associates have accepted him at his word."

Nicholas grimaced but then nodded. "You are correct to consider the counterattacks of the enemy and their defenses."

"When it comes to my declaration that I am Susannah Stanley, I would be immediately refuted by the collective testimony of my so-called family of stepmother and stepsisters." She shuddered at the looming threats. "And my distant cousin who inherited Dalegarth Hall would only be able to recall several brown-haired girls who were easily mistaken for each other even back then." Tears blurred her vision as she looked up the valley toward her old home. "The village was small to begin with and many of the residents already aged. I doubt I was memorable enough for them to be certain enough of my identity six years after we moved away."

Mrs. Jennings shifted on the bench beside her. "What you say holds merit. You have your mother's look about you, and yet while

I wondered at our first meeting, I too easily discarded my suspicions."

If only the woman had pressed for the truth instead of believing her to be a spy. Susannah brushed aside the hurt and instead pressed forward with another counter argument. "And while that may be true, you also are a servant who could have been paid to conveniently remember whatever your master wished."

Silence descended for a few moments, then she presented her final point. "However, if a certain local baronet was to make a statement on my behalf..."

"Of course, I will." Nicholas made the statement with such fervor the others chuckled.

She smiled. "I know this with certainty. Which is why you must first be declared the rightful baronet."

He paced across the terrace again. "Agreed. Now what proof do I have other than my own word and those of...servants." His shoulders slumped. "I grew up in that castle and know every nook and cranny. Unfortunately, my shipmates loved to hear stories and I fear I may have told too much about the lay of the land."

She felt his discouragement as if it were her own. "And then he has been here for months to discover even more. However, like your father's letter that I saved, do you have any correspondence?"

Harold sat up tall but Nicholas was already shaking his head. "My few letters—including yours acknowledging our betrothal—were lost to me when we were captured by the French. I only escaped their prison with the clothes on my back and days later was in the hands of the pirates."

Harold's eyes widened. "That story alone should offer—"

"Except John was by my side until the pirates separated us. His tale would be the same." He continued to pace and mumble. "What kind of proof do I have of my identity? My father's will. A journal. A copy of my mother's marriage lines." Nicholas shoved a hand through his hair in frustration. "Even my scribblings tucked into the corners of the schoolroom would likely have been thrown out over the years. Or scouted out by the impostor."

"You will not know until you have a look." She clung to hope for his sake.

Mrs. Jennings frowned. "Even if the master and his wife were gone for the day, you cannot simply walk in the front door. We would have to sneak you inside while also avoiding the new butler and housekeeper."

Harold laughed. "I don't suppose there are any secret staircases or tunnels to make things simpler?"

Nicholas cracked a smile. "Parts of the foundation date back to the Romans but nary a tunnel to be found. And you more than most know how often I would have used such a thing to escape my lessons."

Their shared laughter brought to mind her childhood image of a youth on horseback exploring the countryside one last time before his father's return.

Nicholas posed with his hands behind his back like an officer instructing his troops. "We will require a diversion and lookouts. Which means we need allies inside the house that we can trust."

The cook nodded. "I will see to the recruits."

"And I can arrange a diversion." Harold waggled his eyebrows.

Susannah's stomach fluttered at the potential danger to them all but could not decide on an alternate plan.

"Assuming I find some sort of evidence, I still need an audience to present it to." Nicholas looked to her. "Your statement about a baronet verifying your identity holds true for me as well. If only there was an earl or a duke to vouch for me..."

"A duke." She gasped as hope grew. "I met the Duke of Middlesbrough in this very castle on the day your father was promoted."

"You did?" Nicholas seemed surprised.

"You were obviously off to war so he could not aid in your identification other than knowing the tales of your heroics that warranted the honor, but he might remember me."

His eyebrows raised in skepticism. "Those heroics as you say occurred before John joined our ship's crew so they might hold merit, but how is the duke to recall one of many girls he met over the years?"

She hurried on. "At Reverend Brooks' recommendation, I was invited to sing at the ceremony. Of course, my stepmother was first the dressmaker who crafted my gown so she might recall the event in general terms. However, neither she nor my stepsisters would know that I sang about the flowers in the forest." She made eye contact with Nicholas and memories stretched between them. She swallowed hard. "The duke got tears in his eyes and complimented me directly."

"Should we ever gain an audience with his grace, your story would help." Nicholas paced another two lengths, then turned to Harold. "You said Reverend Brooks is now a bishop serving the area? If he were to return, he would certainly recall my antics during services and likely Susannah as well if he was the one to recommend her voice."

The earlier seed of hope began to bloom.

Nicholas continued to pace, lost in thought. After a bit, he paused to look over the valley...then turned on his heel with a growing smile. "I was hired to create a garden fit to attract nobles, so what if a few I had known as a child came to see our new terrace...?"

Mrs. Jennings nodded. "You would need the steward's help to get their agreement, but I could see them hosting a small gathering since they are at half-mourning."

Nicholas nodded. "And he should be able to influence the guest list as well, but I could imagine a visit from the Earl of Keswick or even a duke would flatter their twisted desire for attention."

Harold hummed. "You're going to fight this battle using a garden?"

"One considers all possibilities in a war. And while one war is over, another is just beginning." Nicholas clenched his fists at his sides. "I would like nothing more than to stomp up there and confront John face to face. But such an encounter could quickly descend to violence. He basically left me for dead once, and like you said, he has replaced enough servants that I could see him summoning his men to toss me out."

Susannah twisted her hands in her apron. Until Nicholas gained the support of influential allies, his life could be in danger.

Nicholas stopped in front of her. "And I have more to consider than my own wellbeing. I must be here to protect you."

"Me?" Her voice squeaked in a suddenly tight throat.

"If desperate, what is to keep your stepsister from revealing your true identity? Or John from using you as leverage against me?" He shook his head. "There is no telling what he might do. That is why we must bring our potential allies here where they can see the truth for themselves before coming to our aid."

The vicar of her childhood knew of both her scar and her song, but neither could be proven with a letter alone.

She nodded her agreement and the others launched into a discussion about how to convince the steward to their side.

Harold jumped to his feet. "I can invite Mr. Ellis to the stable to discuss our grain storage for the horses. And if Mrs. Jennings is also there—"

"Our testimony as servants may not hold weight with the law, but we had worked together under your father's leadership for several years. He should believe us enough to surely convince him of the truth."

Susannah tried to suppress her doubts, but so much of their plan depended on the steward's cooperation when he could easily side with the impostor.

"He did look at me strangely the day I was hired." Nicholas stroked his bearded chin, then grinned. "I will need to shave this beard before the guests arrive to aid their memories, but in the meantime, I do not think it would be difficult to recall my father's particular habits and preferences as evidence. Those are things I never shared with anyone including John."

A thoughtful gleam sparkled in Nicholas' brown eyes as if additional plans were forming. If the man had his way, soon Muncaster would be overrun with nobility.

But surely such an event could tempt Susan to invite her family to attend. And until Susannah came of legal age, her stepmother still held sway over her future.

A chill of foreboding traveled up her spine and she shivered.

She already knew the depths the woman would go to in her greed. But seeing Nicholas restored to his rightful place would be reward enough no matter the personal cost.

Nicholas must have noticed her fear, for he took her shaking hands in his and stared into her eyes. "Do you trust me?"

She swallowed hard, then whispered, "I do."

With her heart...and with her life.

Nicholas stretched his tight neck muscles and looked up from last year's ledgers laid open on the small wooden desk Harold had helped him move into his room above the stables.

The space was crowded with the additional furniture, but still larger than his shared cabin on the ship or sleeping in a tent during the war. Then again, no matter how often the stalls are cleaned, the aroma of horse droppings permeated everything.

He chuckled. Thankfully, he spent most of his days working out of doors, otherwise Susannah would wrinkle her pretty nose at his stench during their few stolen moments together.

He needed to clear up the question of his identity soon for both their sakes, for parting at the end of the day grew more difficult every time.

However, it should not be long now.

A knock came at the door. "Sir Nicholas? I have come with the invitations."

"Enter." He rose to greet Mr. Ellis and directed him to place the box of parchment on the desk.

The steward had been most relieved to discover his suspicions about Nicholas were correct and quite eager to lend his aid in bringing justice. While equally thrilled to educate Nicholas on the running of the household.

Thankfully, John had little interest in the mundane workings of the estate and had delegated much to the steward who in turn had been relieved to find a more active participant in the true baronet. Hence the ledgers that had allowed Nicholas detailed insight into his father's many business ventures.

He offered the steward the desk chair while he sat on the bed. "How goes the planning?"

Despite a thorough search, they had not uncovered any written evidence inside the castle. Whether it was due to the passage of time or a document purge by the impostor himself, the party invitations held even more importance now.

The steward folded his hands and began his report. "I seem to have aroused a sleeping dragon for the lady of the house presents a new demand every day."

Nicholas cringed at the mention of the additional impostor. "Demands?"

Mr. Ellis grimaced. "First there were additions to the guest list which I had to counter with the argument of space. Then came the hiring of temporary staff to ready the guest rooms and decorate them appropriately. Not to mention the purchase of additional place settings for the dinner party to precede the morning's garden reveal."

Nicholas allowed himself a small smile. With his guidance, the steward had delivered a well-placed strategic compliment about the new terrace implying the nearby Earl of Keswick would be delighted to see the improvements. The couple had taken the bait, and now, in less than a month's time, Muncaster Castle would host a full week of entertainment beginning with a weekend dinner party and formal tour of the grounds.

All so they could take credit for something Nicholas had truly created for himself.

For *his* property.

"And now…" Mr. Ellis withdrew a list from the top of the box. "Now she is wishing there was time to install a fountain and hedge maze on the front lawn."

"Never." He sucked in a quick breath at the travesty. "The view of the castle's facade from the west is certainly impressive but such a manicured arrangement more suitable in London would mar the natural beauty of Cumbria."

"Agreed, my lord. But in the interest of time, I believe I may have diverted her schemes toward new plantings around the base of the walls instead. If that pleases you…" The steward frowned as if he had overstepped.

"Do not worry, Ellis. We are both in an awkward predicament at present." He paused to consider the idea. "Such a notion would easily brighten the look of the castle at large… However, I fear that even with this dreadful beard, personally working that closely to the windows of the study and drawing room might attract attention to my person too soon."

The steward looked at his list. "I understand, but what if you were to hire another gardener to do the work? After all, your current position will need filling." The man smirked.

Nicholas laughed. "It will indeed. See to it my good man." He waved a hand toward the parchment. "Have you been able to rehire the other positions?"

A satisfactory gleam sparked in the man's eye. "Both Mr. Gibbs and Mrs. Richards have readily agreed to return a week before the party and have quietly been made aware of the unique circumstances."

He smiled to know his father's old butler and housekeeper would have their livings restored. He could not blame their current replacements who had taken the positions in good faith, but he was eager to set his household in order with those loyal to his family.

"What other progress?"

The steward worked his way down the list gaining his approval for additional expenditures such as stocking the larder with a secondary order for perishable goods once the true number of guests was established.

At long last, Mr. Ellis turned his attention to the box of folded parchment he had brought with him. "The invitations are addressed but as you suggested, I left room for a personal note. The wax and seal are here as well."

How many times had he seen letters with his father's seal leave Muncaster in the past?

He pushed aside the memory. "Thank you. I will see to it they are posted by morning."

After the steward left, Nicholas reclaimed his chair at the desk. He opened the ink pot and retrieved the first invitation addressed to the Earl of Keswick.

The man was his father's closest friend from their school days and had been a frequent visitor. He smiled at the memory of their frequent jokes over many a dinner that the earl had a title but the Penningtons' had the better castle.

Nicholas dipped the quill and began to write. *Your title may still be grander, but I have managed to improve upon my father's castle and would value your opinion.*

That should serve to remind the earl of their shared history along with a hint at something John would never know.

He set the parchment aside to dry before sealing it and turned to the next in the stack.

The Duke of Middlesbrough.

This time he had to draw upon his father's letter and Susannah's memory of the event for inspiration.

I regret that I was occupied elsewhere during your last visit to Muncaster Castle, but should you be able to attend, this time I shall regale you with the true tale of my part in the Battle of San Domingo.

That story was another bit of information John might have heard spoken of in general terms onboard the Superb from some of the other members of the ship's crew.

From men who had also heard his tales of Muncaster and the valley while overseas but were likely now returned home after the conflict and able to come for a visit.

Men who could identify John at first glance.

Oh, to contemplate such complete justice.

Nicholas made a note to have the steward reserve a few overflow rooms at the Ravenglass Inn, then began to pen a few additional invitations.

Chapter Fifteen

Ine week before their illustrious guests were to arrive, the household was in an uproar of deep cleaning from top to bottom.

Which explained why Susannah was in the butler's pantry near the kitchen polishing a mountain of silver place settings, candelabras, and tea trays alongside a new staff member that Mrs. Jennings had introduced as Mr. Gibbs, the previous butler.

From the twinkle in the man's eye—the same expression she recalled from the baronet ceremony years ago—he was eager to resume his former place as head of the male servants but also enjoying the subterfuge of the current situation.

The man likely believed it inevitable that Nicholas would soon have the authority to release the impostor's hires with severance payments.

Please God, let this house party be used to restore Nicholas to his proper position. Let justice be done.

After all their efforts, she would hate to see Nicholas' hopes dashed when he had already survived so much.

Please, God...

She rubbed her cloth furiously over the tray in her lap.

Mr. Ellis stepped into the small room for a discussion with Mr. Gibbs about the anticipated arrival of a proper wardrobe for the baronet.

In the guise of ordering new clothing for the current occupant of the upper floor and fresh uniforms for the staff, the two men had taken it upon themselves to outfit Nicholas as well. After all, they were the ones placing the orders and orchestrating the payments.

She could hardly wait to see Nicholas in gentleman's clothing.

And yet, she truly enjoyed seeing him in more relaxed working attire.

Susannah glanced at her own maid's uniform and recalled the few dresses she had brought with her months ago. The only one worthy to be worn as his future wife was her burgundy gown from Pru's debut, for the others were not only castoff day dresses from Susan but they had also been worn daily for housework in Liverpool.

If only she could secure new garments as well...but that would come in time. Hopefully.

And yet, the closer Nicholas came to his reinstatement, the more she felt like an anchor holding him back.

She took her frustrations out on a fork.

"Easy there, my darling, or there will be no silver left to eat from." Nicholas' deep voice in her ear sent tingles spreading fast over her skin and heat rushing to her face.

The other two men bowed as proper but still chuckled.

Thankfully, Nicholas turned his attention to the steward. "Any additional attendees I should be aware of?"

After learning of Nicholas' surprise additions to the guest list, the steward was screening the responses.

"Two from your former ship—a Captain Drake and a Benjamin Lewis—will be attending and I have secured rooms for them in town."

A satisfied smile grew on Nicholas' face. "I look forward to our reunion."

The men had been through much together and were truer friends to the rightful baronet than most of the nobles or merchants rounding out the original guest list.

People she was ill-suited to mingle with.

She set aside the polished fork and awkwardly straightened her apron before reaching for another utensil.

Nicholas rested a hand on her shoulder as if to reassure her.

"And..." The steward's face was practically glowing. "We have heard from Middlesbrough that he is looking forward to meeting such a hero. Something about you saving even more lives recently?"

Nicholas squirmed beside her but she grinned along with the others. It appeared what Nicholas had told her about his additional note in the duke's invitation had sparked the proper memory of that event so many years ago.

Hopefully the duke would remember her as well.

Mr. Ellis cleared his throat. "However, his grace also mentioned it is time to add Sir Nicholas to the Official Roll as a belated formality. Making the timing of this weekend's revelations even more important."

Beside her, Nicholas rocked on his feet. Once the guests arrived, he planned to first approach the Earl of Keswick privately and then use each additional ally to sway the rest over the course of several days.

She set down her cloth and pressed a hand over her churning stomach as the worries assailed her.

What if they were caught and banished before getting the chance?

Or worse, what if he was not recognized or believed?

"Susannah, will you do me the honor of a walk in the garden? It seems you could do with a bit of fresh air."

She glanced up to find the steward had already departed, leaving only a grinning Mr. Gibbs to pretend he was more interested in the silver than the couple. While she was glad for friends and allies in the household, the meddling busybodies could get tiresome.

Making any excuse to escape a welcome one.

She nodded and a few minutes later strolled beside Nicholas along the paths of the kitchen gardens listening to his animated musings about how best to approach the earl or if he should reunite with the naval officers first.

There was so much that could go wrong that she could not fathom all the possibilities.

As he continued to debate the possibilities, they took a seat on the shaded bench in the corner amidst the bluebells that also bloomed wildly elsewhere on the castle grounds.

It was the very spot where they had first shared a romantic interlude.

Her face heated at the memories, but her fears resurfaced.

Once Nicholas was no longer a sailor or gardener, would he still want her?

Or worse, would he even be able to keep her?

"You are too quiet, my love. What troubles you?"

She shifted to face him. "I know not how, but I have no doubt you will be restored to your rightful place." She drew in a shaky breath. "But what of their marriage? What if Susan is married not to John, but to the baronet? To the person holding the title? What would become of me then?"

He clasped her hand as if to offer comfort, then frowned. "We must seek answers from the church. And quickly." He stood and pulled her up beside him. "I must write another letter."

Susannah added a handful of pea pods to her basket then moved on to harvest from the next plant. The task kept her hands busy, but did nothing to ease her awareness that the first guests were due to arrive within a few hours with dinner scheduled for six o'clock that evening.

She glanced across to where a now beardless and inherently more handsome Nicholas weeded the beds from an adjacent path. A procession of emotions flitted across his face as he hacked the ground with his hoe.

"Stefan?" She pivoted to see Harold striding towards them from the stables.

It felt odd to hear Nicholas called by that name, but they never knew when someone else might be eavesdropping. The necessary ruse chafed, but they could not risk being exposed prematurely.

"There is a message for you from town." Harold handed over a folded piece of parchment. "I will await your response."

Her heart galloped at the sight of the elaborate seal.

Nicholas broke the wax and then read it silently. After a quick glance around, he beckoned her closer. "The bishop—Reverend Brooks—arrived in Ravenglass last eve and is staying at the current vicar's lodgings." He shook the note in his hand. "He received my—Sir Nicholas'—letter and now wishes to speak with the gardener Stefan."

She nodded. Nicholas had been very careful with the wording of his letter in case the message was intercepted by individuals on either end of the exchange.

"We are to appear within the hour."

She gasped, then looked down at her dirty hands and apron.

"You've little time." Nicholas folded away the note. "Meet me in the stable courtyard in ten minutes."

Harold stepped away, then turned toward the stables. "I'll ready a wagon."

As she scurried toward the kitchens, she had a vague sense of Nicholas protesting and something about picking up a delivery while they were in town. But her mind had leapt ahead to seeing their old vicar again.

While they hoped the man would recognize and support them both, now that the moment had arrived, her stomach churned.

With the half-filled basket of vegetables on her arm, she slipped inside the kitchen door, then stopped abruptly at the sight of Mrs. Finch talking to Mrs. Jennings.

Lately she had managed to avoid the housekeeper altogether. After all, the stern woman had taken pleasure in waving around the indenture papers and demoting Susannah to the kitchens. Not to mention that while looking in the study for any papers to prove Nicholas' identity, they had been unable to locate that contract...leaving them to wonder if the document was still in the housekeeper's possession.

Who knew what the woman was capable of?

But Susannah could not risk getting into trouble now. Not so close to the dinner party and the culmination of Nicholas' plans.

She lowered her head and pretended she had been sent on a harvesting errand rather than reassigned to assist the gardener. After setting her basket on the worktable, she murmured something about the plants not being ready to harvest completely, then crossed the room to wash her hands. She quickly splashed water on her face and donned a clean apron as if readying to continue the food preparations.

However, Mrs. Finch lingered and time was ticking by.

With her heart in her throat, she maneuvered herself behind the housekeeper and made eye contact with Mrs. Jennings. She quickly made the sign of the cross and prayed the woman recalled their desire to meet with the bishop.

The cook gave a slight nod, then subtly shifted her own position, gradually moving toward another area of the kitchen...until finally the housekeeper's back was turned to the exit.

Susannah slipped out the door and ran down the path toward the stables.

When she arrived, Nicholas frowned at her dirt-stained maid's uniform beneath the fresh apron.

"I am sorry, but Mrs. Finch was in the kitchen and I had to sneak out again rather than change completely." She took his hand as he helped her up to the wagon seat.

"It cannot be helped." He hurried around to join her, then flicked the reins, setting the horses into motion.

By the time she had caught her breath, Nicholas had already shifted his focus to the coming conversation. "Let me do the talking. Once our identities are confirmed, then we can seek answers regarding the validity of their marriage, especially as it pertains to us."

Susannah gripped the wagon seat tightly. So much could go wrong today.

Nicholas obviously noticed her plight, for he shifted toward her. "What is the matter?"

"What if he doesn't recognize me?" Her greatest fear burst from her lips. "Susan and I both lived here, both have brown hair, both have grown up, and often had our names mixed up even before this. Not to mention I'm dressed like a maid with indenture papers in the hands of another. And if my stepmother caught wind of this, she could still have me committed and locked away for my supposed delusions."

Nicholas rested a calming hand on her arm.

She drew in a deep breath. "Forgive my panic. I was nervous enough about seeing the bishop before almost getting caught by

Mrs. Finch. Because in our current position, you can do nothing if she chose to punish me."

"I could. And I would."

The steely determination in his voice allowed her to relax as the wagon drew closer to town.

Nicholas lowered his voice. "We are in a war fighting for justice and truth. But like every conflict, not every skirmish may go in your favor. You simply survive to fight another day while knowing you have fellow soldiers by your side."

She caught the hint of nostalgia and loss in his voice for he knew firsthand about battles.

She pressed a hand over his, then shifted away from him on the seat, allowing the proper distance and bowing her head toward her lap. If the villagers paid attention, they would only see a maid.

Mere minutes later, Nicholas parked the wagon outside the resident vicar's house and helped her down. He led the way toward the door, then knocked.

A servant opened the door, then after Nicholas announced their intent, they were told to wait in the entryway.

Before long, the man they were seeking exited a room down the hall and strode toward them. His eyes swept upward over Nicholas' workman's clothes. "You must be Ste—" He gasped. "Nicholas? By all that's holy, Sir Nicholas Pennington dressed as a commoner? I confess my confusion..." The bishop's mouth opened and shut as he staggered toward them.

"You confess? Usually *I* was the one confessing." Nicholas laughed.

Relieved he had been so readily identified, she stepped to his side, drawing attention to herself.

"And you brought a maid..." Reverend Brooks' eyes widened even further to the point of bulging. "Miss Susannah Stanley?" He collapsed onto a nearby chair and waved a weak hand at the two of them.

A weight fell from her shoulders. He knew her at a glance even before bringing up any past memories. She grinned at the bishop, then up at Nicholas.

"I heard you were married but why the..." The bishop gestured to their clothes.

"*We* are not married. Yet." Nicholas winked, and her pulse skittered at the implied promise.

"Then who...? What...?" The bishop's confusion turned grim as if finally realizing that some injustice had been done. "What has transpired while I was away on church business?"

"That is a long story." Nicholas glanced around the entryway.

Before he could continue, the bishop stood. "Follow me to the study where we can have privacy." He turned back toward the room he had come from. "I would like Reverend Edwards to also join us and help shed light on the situation."

She took Nicholas' arm and followed along on shaky legs.

A half hour later, Nicholas wrapped up his summary of where each of them had been in the intervening years and how they came to be servants at the castle while others had usurped their positions.

Throughout his explanation, the local vicar—Reverend Edwards—had nodded as if recognizing the truth. Although the man's ready acceptance could have been due to his bishop's obvious belief and interjected questions, it was a relief to have gained yet another ally.

Reverend Brooks folded his hands atop the desk as if it were still his home. "And now what are your plans? For you cannot continue thus."

Nicholas rubbed the back of his neck. "Actually, I have a plan to reclaim my position beginning later today with the arrival of guests for a garden party at Muncaster." He glanced at Susannah in the chair beside him, then back to the clergy. "Your ready identification of my person has bolstered my belief that my fellow sailors and my childhood memories of the Earl of Keswick will help to convince the Duke of Middlesbrough of my identity as well."

The bishop nodded. "If I might also be of assistance with the duke, send word."

"I thank you." At least the man did not think his plans were far-fetched.

"And I on his behalf, but..." Susannah's soft voice wavered.

He would do anything to see her happy and safe, including broach a sensitive topic. "There is another matter we wished to discuss." He cleared his throat. "Once reinstated, am I unencumbered to claim my true bride?"

The clergy exchanged confused glances.

He leaned forward. "Susannah and I have been betrothed for many a year, but before we could be reunited and kindle the spark ignited as children—"

"*They* married using our names." Her voice shook. "Are *we* married? Or are *they*? Or is my stepsister married to the real baronet once he is identified?" Her voice cracked.

If only he could ease her fears.

Despite their audience, he reached out to clasp her hand. "What does the church—and the law—say about marriage...by proxy?" Was he bungling the explanation?

The bishop was the first to respond. "Where were the banns read and the ceremony held?"

Susannah cleared her throat. "The ceremony was held in Liverpool closer to the bride's friends and in deference to the groom's supposed mourning to not have a lavish reception here. As to the banns, I know they were read in Liverpool, but I was locked away in my room and the bishop there had already been warned by my stepmother of my supposed delusions. Not to mention, in all our years living there, he ever only knew me by the shortened version of my name, Anna."

The local vicar rubbed his chin. "There were banns read here as well, but I have never met the baronet's returned—presumed—son in person. Due to his injuries and grief—" He coughed and looked down. "I sent my curate to deliver communion and take confession to assure his privacy. 'Tis a practice he still prefers."

And the very reason Nicholas had been able to attend services himself, even if he was relegated to the edges to preserve his own privacy.

Reverend Brooks tapped a finger against his lips. "Marriage by proxy is rare indeed and usually only for royal brides from other countries until they can arrive on English soil and present themselves in the church." He paused as if in thought. "I assume they did not represent themselves as proxies but rather spoke your names and not their own during the ceremony and signed the register with your names as well?"

Susannah shifted on her chair. "I would think so. However, I know not for certain since I was not allowed to attend—for obvious reasons—and was in fact already here at Muncaster. While Nicholas—"

"Was still somewhere in Spain trying to work my way home." His mind spun in circles with his many questions. "Does not the marriage law require each party to give their consent?"

"Aye." A smile grew on Reverend Edward's face as if he could already guess where Nicholas' mind was leading.

He nodded. "That is good. Because I did not and do not consent to marry the woman who appeared in that church."

"Nor I...to the impostor." Susannah stumbled over her words. "Does that mean we are both free?"

The bishop nodded with authority from behind the desk. "I see no reason why not for neither of you were present nor gave consent for a proxy to stand in your place." He turned to the local vicar seated on another chair nearby. "As for the other individuals...? I will inquire with my superiors as to the validity of a marriage under such pretext where both parties sought to misrepresent and deceive the other, but will also need to send a letter to the Liverpool parish explaining the circumstances and instructing them to strike the registry."

"Agreed." Reverend Edwards rose and pulled a stack of fresh parchment from a drawer. "The magistrates will also need to be informed."

"I believe the Earl of Keswick can see to the legal matters but I will write him as well."

Nicholas cleared his throat to get their attention. "The earl is arriving at Muncaster this afternoon for a week's stay if you wish to address him there."

The bishop smiled. "That will be most convenient."

Nicholas sat back in his chair with relief, then eyed Susannah beside him. "Now that we are officially unencumbered in the eyes of the church, will you marry me?"

A burst of startled laughter escaped her lips before she smiled. "Of course I will."

The bishop laughed as well. "When shall I read the banns?"

Susannah paled, her gaze darting between his and the clergy. "I am not of age and my stepmother could still prohibit the union."

"Is not your father's distant cousin your guardian? Or would that have been my father..." His voice trailed off at the realization that announcing such a thing prematurely would certainly alert John to Susannah's existence.

Her voice quivered. "If you are unable to reclaim your title soon, I fear we shall have to wait until September to wed."

He shook his head. "Their deception continues to punish us for I am powerless to protect you." He rubbed his thumb over the back of her hand that he still held. "How am I ever to forgive if something were to happen to you in the meantime?"

She rested her free hand atop their joined hands. "The earl is coming as well as your captain." She glanced at the concerned clergymen. "And we now have allies in the church. I pray we do not have to wait much longer."

The tension in his muscles eased. "Such wisdom." Over her shoulder, he spied the time on the mantel clock. The first guests would be arriving within the hour.

He released her hand and stood, then nodded to the clergy. "We thank you for your audience and support, but if we are to continue our masquerade as servants for the time being, we must get back to the castle posthaste."

Susannah rose with a gasp. After offering a quick goodbye, she headed for the door.

"I will be praying for you both." The bishop reached for a quill. "In the meantime, I will start on those inquiries now."

Reverend Edwards trailed behind Nicholas toward the entryway as if seeing them all the way out. "It is unfortunate you don't live in Scotland..."

Nicholas paused his retreat and turned to see the man with a twinkle in his eye.

The vicar shrugged. "Their laws are different and one could get married right away."

No banns. No minimum age.

Just a relatively short trip north across the border to Gretna Green.

His smile grew. "I thank you for your wisdom should circumstances not unfold in our favor." A laugh escaped. "However, if this goes according to plan, I believe the banns will need reading soon."

"I would be delighted."

And his dream to marry Susannah in the castle's chapel would be realized.

On light feet, he rushed to join her, more than eager for the weekend's events to get underway.

Chapter Sixteen

Susannah leaned forward on the rough seat, silently urging the horses to go faster on their return trip to Muncaster. So much depended on a successful dinner party and Mrs. Jennings would need her hands in the kitchen.

As Nicholas turned their loaded wagon through the gate into the stable courtyard, the place was astir with several new carriages parked to one side and a few strangers milling about. Probably the drivers and the footmen of the guests.

Her stomach fluttered with excitement to see all their planning for the event beginning to bear fruit.

Nicholas steered the horses to a spot near the footpath to the castle for easier unloading, but before they had barely stopped, Harold rushed toward them from the stable.

"Thank the Almighty you've returned."

"Quite the welcome, my friend." Nicholas laughed as he secured the reins, then jumped to the ground. "Were you so eager for this delivery?"

"Forgive me, my lord." Nicholas started to protest the address in front of the strangers but Harold barreled on. "The... lady of the castle..." He cast an apologetic glance at her and drew a deep breath. "She must have issued her own invitation for Lady Stanley and her daughter arrived not a half hour past."

Susan's mother. And Pru. Here?

A wave of dizziness had her swaying on the seat.

The woman was already capable of locking Susannah in a room, threatening her freedom, and forging indenture papers. What schemes would she concoct with her daughter's help?

Her breaths were coming faster until Nicholas reached up and grasped her trembling hand in his strong fingers.

Right. How could she have forgotten that she was not alone?

Nicholas helped her to the ground where she leaned on his arm for support.

Harold cleared his throat. "The household is in a scramble to adjust the room assignments to account for the unexpected guests. However, Mrs. Jennings sent me to fetch you and issue the warning that the maid Anna is to finish her duties and then present herself to the mistress's room where she will remain to help them prepare for dinner." Harold tugged on his ear. "Since when did kitchen maids serve as lady's maids?"

Susannah sighed. "So much has happened since my arrival here, that I had put it from my mind. My stepmother's original intent was that I serve her daughter in that role. As if to continue to punish me for some unknown offense by keeping me in close proximity of all I had been denied."

Harold looked horrified at the woman's vindictiveness, but Nicholas merely squeezed her waist in support.

She drew in a slow breath. "Thankfully, Mrs. Finch did not take kindly to being told how to assign her staff and I was relegated to the kitchens instead. And then apparently elevated to working in the gardens." She shared a smile with Nicholas.

Too soon, reality encroached and her shoulders slumped. "It was a welcome reprieve, but now it seems that I must return to the lion's den to face her wrath in person."

"Could you not deny her summons?" Nicholas had apparently recognized the potential danger.

If only she were free to do just that. "Unless we are prepared to begin the revelations before the rest of your guests arrive, I fear I must at least pretend compliance and cater to their whims." She sighed. "That at least is something I am quite accustomed to over the years."

Nicholas stiffened beside her. "I will speak to the earl or my naval captain as soon as either of them arrives."

Harold shifted on his feet. "I will keep a lookout and send word straightaway."

"Thank you." Nicholas nodded at Harold, then turned back to her. "Until then, perhaps I should find an excuse to linger in the upper halls."

The very place where she had encountered the impostor before. Suddenly she feared for Nicholas' safety more than her own. "But that is where—"

He held a finger to her lips. "The woman locked you in a tower to force her way. I cannot imagine that she has changed much and I would rather be discovered early than risk your harm."

Susannah's knees shook with her relief. She would not be alone in the battle ahead.

After a quick goodbye to Harold, she started down the path toward the castle to face her greatest fears with Nicholas by her side.

The time had come for her to take action. And perhaps she wouldn't be quite as accommodating as her stepmother might have wished.

Susannah tightened her grip on the tray as the familiar voices from her past drifted out from behind the closed door of Susan's private sitting room.

The time had come to... "Speak the truth. No more hiding."

Her whispered words barely caused a stir in the air but Nicholas responded in kind. "Be the woman your parents wanted you to be."

Her father had wanted her to get along with his new wife, but never at such a price. With memories of Dalegarth Hall and a majestic waterfall stirring in her heart, she took a deep breath for courage.

Nicholas, in his ill-fitting borrowed footman's coat, moved his hand to the knob to assist her entrance. "Try to delay any revelations about me, but know that whatever happens, I *will* protect you." The fire of promise blazed in his eyes.

She offered a small smile in return. "I know. After all, your name means victory of the people."

He grinned. "And you only thought to mention that now?"

"Perhaps I needed to remember that God has a bigger plan for us." She pinched her lips together.

Please, let it be so.

She nodded at the door, Nicholas turned the knob, and she stepped into the room. "The castle's cook thought you might enjoy a bit of refreshment to tide you over until dinner."

Her elegantly dressed stepmother rose from the couch with a glare. "How dare you enter without knocking? Is that the sort of uncouth training this household allows?"

Susannah held a steady pace as she crossed the room to deposit the heavy tray on the low table situated between the two chairs.

"Susan, dear, you really must learn to take a firmer hand with your staff."

The lady of the house huffed. "Mother, really. You sent for Anna, did you not?"

"Anna?"

Of course, her dear stepmother would be unable to see past the uniform to notice the person who wore it. Her loss.

Susannah smoothed a hand over her clean dress and turned with a forced smile. "Would you care for me to pour?"

Lady Stanley's eyes widened in recognition, then narrowed. "Ladies maids do not wear uniforms nor damage their hands with menial work. How else are you to avoid snagging the delicate fabrics of your sister's gowns or properly style her hair?"

She shifted slightly to catch Susan's nod toward the teapot while Pru was already reaching for the assortment of sweets. At least serving tea would give her hands something to do.

Midway through pouring the first cup—while enduring a continued lecture—she noticed that the door was slightly ajar. Meaning Nicholas could hear every word of the woman's rant.

She fought to contain her smile as she delivered Susan's tea but it was noticed by the older woman.

"Do you mock me?"

"No, ma'am." She concentrated on pouring a cup for Pru. "I just find it interesting that you know so much about the proper behavior of a lady's maid when none of us ever had that luxury either here in Boot or in Liverpool." She delivered Pru's cup and turned to her stepmother with a raised eyebrow. "Unless you were able to afford one in Carlile on a dressmaker's income?"

The older woman huffed and collapsed into a chair. "I wanted better for my daughter and who better to anticipate her needs than you."

"However, the housekeeper deemed my services were better utilized elsewhere and I have enjoyed my work in the kitchen and gardens." Susannah reached for the final cup on the tray.

"You would be the type..." Her stepmother mumbled something about changing her future role.

She pursed her lips to keep from smiling as she delivered the last of the tea and set about straightening the room. Little did the woman know what role Susannah would soon fill if God granted Nicholas favor.

After adjusting the window curtains to let in more of the afternoon light, she glanced into the adjoining room and noticed that several dresses were already laid out for dinner. She should probably check them for wrinkles before it got too late.

Behind her, Susan giggled. "I never imagined a duke would ever come to my castle to see my gardens."

Her gardens?

It wasn't Susan's castle. And the idea for upgrading the garden had come from Susannah.

Susan sighed. "I wonder if Middlesbrough will be impressed or sneer at our humble halls."

"He has been here before." The words escaped her lips before she could suppress them. Too much time spent among the staff alone and around Nicholas had taught her to speak her mind without social constraints.

"What?"

"When?"

"And how would you know?"

She turned to find Susan sputtering, Pru staring with a cake suspended halfway to her lips, and her stepmother turning red in the face.

Despite feeling bold with the truth, it would be prudent to skirt around the details. How ever was she to survive their scrutiny for the hours until Nicholas could speak to the first of his special guests?

"You will answer. What do you know of the duke?" Lady Stanley returned her cup to the tray and clenched her fists in her lap until her knuckles whitened.

Susannah swallowed hard. "The duke was the king's representative when Sir Thomas was elevated to baronet. My father and I were invited to the ceremony and you—" She nodded to the woman. "You met my father when we traveled to Carlile to order a new dress for the occasion."

A flash of memory sparked in the woman's eyes, followed swiftly by a calculating gleam as she pressed for more details. "Tell us everything you remember about your interactions with the other guests, especially the duke."

It was just like before when they had discovered she had been betrothed to the heir of this very castle and pressed for every advantage. Except this time she could not risk letting another bit of information about the duke escape.

How else was she to prove herself if given the opportunity?

Her knowledge was a weapon...to be wielded later.

She clamped her lips shut and turned back toward the adjoining room. "I need to see to your dresses for this evening."

"Stop!"

Susannah flinched at the rage in her stepmother's tone, then glanced over her shoulder to see the woman was on her feet.

"You *will* tell us about that event."

"What are you hiding?" Susan also stood, giving Pru the opportunity to shove another cake into her mouth without reprimand. "Are you keeping more secrets from us?" She crossed her arms over her chest and glared.

"It happened years ago." Susannah's voice wavered and she forced strength back into her tone. "I don't see how—"

"You don't see?" Her stepmother advanced quickly and Susannah backed away toward the window. "You little fool. I should have had you locked far away while I had the chance."

Susannah tried to dart past her toward the hall, but the woman reached out a hand and clamped onto her arm, fingernails digging into her skin.

She wiggled but could not break free. "Let me go!"

"Never!" Her stepmother screamed, spittle flying. "You will continue to pay for your father's neglect."

Neglect? The woman had gone mad and based on the silence of her daughters, there would be no support from that quarter.

"Help!"

Nicholas immediately appeared in the doorway and took in the scene. "Unhand her at once."

Her captor spun toward the door but her grip never lessened. "Who are you to instruct me?" She lifted her nose in the air. "You are just a footman and a filthy one at that."

Nicholas took a menacing step closer as if to force the woman into compliance.

With one last vicious squeeze, her stepmother released her grip and backed away. "Someone! Help us!"

Surely her voice carried out into the hall, but Nicholas ignored them, simply stepping closer and sweeping his gaze over her form. Susannah rubbed her wounded arm, but nodded that she was well.

"What is the meaning of such unladylike behavior?" The tall stranger she had seen so many months before entered the room with a condescending sneer aimed at his wife and her relatives. "Do not dare sully my name before—" He saw Nicholas. "You."

"Me." Nicholas smiled. "Imagine my surprise to find you here?"

John's bloodshot eyes darted about the room. "You are mad. Remove yourself at once or I shall call to have you removed."

"No." Nicholas folded his arms and stood his ground.

Such calm in the face of provocation.

Meanwhile, the other women appeared to be in shock as they compared two similar but very different men.

"In my wife's private chambers? How dare you?" John had to be bluffing even as he glanced over his shoulder at the door as if awaiting the arrival of reinforcements...or planning his escape.

"Your wife? Interesting." Nicholas drawled as if bored. "When were you planning to tell her the truth?"

John rushed forward and flew a fist toward Nicholas' face.

Nicholas simply ducked down, then leveraged his shoulder into the other man's chest, sending the man's limbs flying.

Susannah tried to back away from the altercation, but somehow tripped over a footstool and fell against a side table, yelping at the sudden pain in her hip.

Nicholas turned as if to help her but was blindsided by another blow and fell to the carpet face first.

"Nicholas!" She scrambled to place herself between the men.

Susan rushed to her husband's side and tugged on his sleeve. "Yes, Nicholas, let our servants throw out the riffraff."

Her stepmother sniffed. "No need to get your hands dirty."

But Susannah's words had attracted John's direct attention and he narrowed his eyes with venom in his voice. "What did you call him?"

She realized her error and quickly glanced at the real Nicholas who was now blinking and shaking his head as if coming round. She needed to gain time for him to recover.

She slowly rose to her feet but kept her head down as if she were a true maid. No sense in riling the villain further when every moment mattered.

John shook her shoulders. "Answer me, you worthless wench. Who is this man to you?" Spittle flew in her face and she felt more than heard movement behind her at her feet.

She slowly lifted her eyes and declared the truth. "He is mine."

A chuckle behind her was followed by the heat of his full height at her back. Nicholas forcibly removed John's hands from her shoulders. "And if you back-stabbing, sucker-punching fraud ever lay another finger on her person, you will know the true meaning of pain."

If she thought John erratic before, she was mistaken.

For before she could comprehend his intent, the look of a cornered animal—the same as the rabid fox from years ago—dropped into his eyes. He took one step back, then turned to lunge for the door.

In a flash, Nicholas pushed around her and tackled the man to the floor.

Susan screamed as more blows were exchanged.

From her vantage, John tried to dislodge Nicholas in order to make an escape while Nicholas sought to hold him captive long enough to make him answer for his crimes.

But as the violence spilled out into the hallway, she feared the outcome.

Dear God, bring him help. Enact justice.

She followed the noise and the other women into the carpeted corridor as the altercation moved toward the stairs. Beyond the scrambling men, she spotted the shocked faces of a few servants and several richly attired ladies.

Oh dear. Their revelation plans had veered far from the plan.

Then appearing at the top of the stairs was Mr. Ellis. "Sir Nicholas? What is—"

"Just in time to help me constrain him, good man."

Once outnumbered, John's actions became even more frantic and he reached toward his boot.

Susannah spied the handle in his hand and screamed. "A knife!"

Nicholas somehow twisted and kicked the weapon out of his grasp and it flew over the railing before finally clattering on the marble floor below.

At least it had not injured anyone.

But John was not going quietly.

He landed a low punch on the steward's side, causing him to lose his grip, then rushed down the stairs as if seeking to reclaim his weapon.

Or seeking the exit.

Dear God, no!

Nicholas and the steward disappeared down the stairs after him and Susannah rushed forward to watch the outcome.

Harold emerged from the shadows and within moments, he had John's arm twisted high behind his back and the knife kicked further across the floor spinning toward the opening front door where a flash of blue coats signaled the arrival of two men in naval uniform.

In a matter of heartbeats, Susannah registered the number of ladies gathered alongside her at the railing—including her step-mother and stepsisters—as well as additional curiosity-seekers emerging below from the drawing room where she knew the staff had laid out a light buffet of refreshments for the arriving guests.

In the stunned silence of the tableau, Nicholas stalked down the remainder of the stairs and approached the impostor.

"Sir Nicholas?" The older of the two sailors glanced with confusion at Nicholas' torn footman's jacket and John's equally disheveled—but regal—clothing.

"Who is this brigand?" Another man spoke from near the drawing room door. "And why is my old friend's son dressed as a—"

"Silence!" A somewhat familiar man with a natural authority pushed past the others and strode into the middle of the chaos. "What is the meaning of this?"

A choked gasp crossed her lips. "Your grace..." What a horrible first impression when seeking the man's favor and influence to right the wrongs.

Nicholas glanced her direction, then quickly turned back to execute a flawless bow before removing his borrowed jacket. "I had not planned it this way, your grace, but...it is past time to unmask the impostors who have taken my castle.

The duke eyed John still desperately trying to escape from Harold's grasp and motioned the military men forward. "Officer? Please help detain him while we move to the drawing room to sort this out."

Chapter Seventeen

Nicholas scanned the drawing room as he followed the duke toward the central seating area.

It was the first time he had seen the space since his return and the memories assaulted him from every side. Visions of where his mother used to sit with her stitching when he was a child mingled with those of his father reading by the fire, his favorite hunting dog at his feet...all superimposed by the present company in all their finery craning their necks to gather the latest gossip.

Behind him, he heard muttered curses and the sounds of an ongoing struggle as John was brought to a chair and forced to sit with Benjamin's beefy hand on his shoulder.

It was so good to see the man alive for more than his current aid and coming testimony as to John's identity.

The duke stood in front of the fireplace, his dignified bearing proof of his rank and graying hair proof of his accumulated wisdom. He hoped.

The man waved Nicholas to a chair opposite the captive, then frowned. "Explain yourself."

The battle had begun and as a Pennington, he would rise to the challenge.

He took a deep breath. "My name is Nicholas Pennington and I grew up within these very walls." He gestured to the inner circle of spectators, spying Susannah and her *family* to his right. "I recall many of you as my father's guests over the years, even though I was more inclined to spend my days out of doors roaming this valley at will. Doing such is how I met Miss Susannah Stanley and her father Sir William in the nearby village of Boot."

He risked another glance at his betrothed in time to catch her smile and her stepmother's glare. He turned back to the duke. "At the age of fifteen, I was sent to sea by my father to learn the shipping trade. A year later, I was impressed into the Royal Navy where I served faithfully for ten years. I have heard it was in this very room that you yourself lauded certain actions I performed in the Battle of San Domingo."

Middlesbrough nodded and others in the room murmured their memories of that event. He caught someone's voice nearby relaying how proud his father had been.

Nicholas suppressed his emotions. There would be time enough later.

Instead, he waved a hand across to the men holding John in place. "I only recall scaling the rigging with a corner of the mainsail as if I were climbing one of our local cliffs, but Captain Drake could tell you the outcome."

"Your grace." His captain bowed his head to the duke. "I am—was—the captain of the Superb. The damage to our mast from a direct hit had turned us off course and we were defenseless. This man's bravery allowed us to catch enough wind to then turn back into the battle where our fleet gained the victory." The man smiled at Nicholas. "He saved my life and that of my crew and it was my honor to promote him and by order of the king, years later to bestow upon him the knighthood."

Nicholas found an answering smile as the proof of his identity mounted.

Thank You, God, for credible witnesses on my behalf.

He glanced around the crowded room noting the nods of many including a few servants at the back of the room, before catching Susannah's proud smile...and the paling faces of the women beside her.

He would deal with them later.

The duke cleared his throat. "Then who is this man and how did he come to be here?"

Captain Drake spoke first. "This man is John Marbury, a seaman on my ship who enlisted a few years ago and was later assigned to Sir Nicholas' crew to help operate one of our cannons on shore as requested to support Wellington's forces."

A murmur grew from somewhere in the crowd. Apparently that part of the story had never been told.

Nicholas faced the duke. "Your grace, there were five men assigned to me including Mr. Benjamin Lewis who is also present." He pointed to the loyal man still holding the scoundrel in place. "Last July, we found ourselves at Maya Pass in the Pyrenees. After the failed attempt to retake the high ground, we used our gun to cover the retreat of the British forces, but were ourselves captured by the French along with others and held in a temporary prison of a barn."

His forehead throbbed with the memory of those dark days and injury. "I helped organize an escape and was the last man outside as I erased the evidence of our path. Except when someone ahead of me accidentally caught the attention of a guard, I chose to act as a decoy to draw the French away from the others. However, John had not yet reached cover—where Benjamin was waiting—and ended up beside me as we ran. Just not fast enough to avoid a bullet through my shoulder." He rubbed his old wound.

"You earned another commendation from Wellington for those heroics." Captain Drake grunted. "I'll see that he knows where to find you."

"When you did not rejoin our forces, I was sure you had perished and John alongside you." Benjamin squeezed the squirming captive's shoulder. "Were you recaptured? And how did you end up here?"

Nicholas grimaced. "It is a long story. After several days roaming the countryside, John and I had evaded the French search parties only to encounter a band of heathen pirates."

Middlesbrough's eyes widened amid other murmurs in the room as Nicholas quickly told how they'd been separated on the ship of hostages, how he'd been sold as a slave, and worked on the docks in Morocco until his eventual escape and slow return across the continent. "I finally arrived here almost two months ago, only to learn that my father was dead and another had inherited. One the villagers claimed was me."

He looked into eyes of his father's friends. "I thought it prudent to gain more information before making myself known and approached the steward about the gardener position he had been recruiting. Of course, despite the ruse and a different name, a few of the servants knew me immediately and have been helping keep me hidden and supporting my quest for justice. Through one of them…" He swallowed at the memory of Susannah's letter. "…I saw the letter in my father's own hand that he had hoped to ransom me from the pirates."

Silence descended in the room, until one spoke up. "How did—John, did you say?—come to be ransomed in your place?"

He clenched his fists. "That is where the deception began. Once we reached Morocco, I told the pirates my name but they only laughed. Probably because John had already given them my name for himself." He glared at the man who refused to look up. "The irony is that one of my fellow slaves—whose name I have been using—chose to help me escape to his own peril...while my name allowed a thief to not only find freedom, but steal my title and castle and bride."

A slight chuckle escaped his lips, and he waved a hand toward Susannah and the other Stanley women. "Well, not *my* bride since apparently John is not the only one with avarice in Cumbria."

Multiple sets of eyes including his shipmates turned toward the women. "The lady is not—"

"Is not the Susannah Stanley who I knew when she was but nine years of age long before our fathers arranged our marriage." He gave her a brief smile, but proving her identity would only come after establishing his own.

He rose to his feet and approached the duke. "After so many years away from home, I knew it would be difficult to prove my identity since it would be his word against mine. And while my loyal servants knew me, I needed more credible witnesses." He waved a hand at the surrounding guests and pivoted to face them. "All of you. I worked with my father's steward to arrange many of your additions to the guest list because you had visited here in the past."

He paused with another smile. "I may have actually gone so far as to point out specific incidents in my own hand to bring those memories to the surface." He deliberately sought out a few familiar faces in succession. "Chess by the fire. The too-small fish you caught in the pond that grew larger as the story was told. Your delight in our cook's desserts. I could go on with more detail if necessary."

Their shocked but nodding reactions only served as further proof of his identity.

All he needed to tip the scales was for the vile man to confess.

"I thought you were my friend." He stalked closer to his former crewman and fought to control his anger. "When we escaped that barn and created the distraction to aid the others, I was relieved not

to be alone. But then...You took my coat and pretended to be me."
He pointed a finger in the man's face. "You lied about your name
when captured the second time. Let yourself be ransomed in my
place. And were even reunited with my father for at least a short
time...before he mysteriously died at the hands of thieves who were
brazen enough to attack in the daylight."

"About that..." The Earl of Keswick stepped forward beside
the duke. "There hadn't been danger to daytime visitors to the
docks in years and a father certainly would have known his own
son." The earl folded his arms over his chest and frowned. "Even if
this man had no intention of continuing his ruse once safely back
on English soil, I would wager the impostor could have seen Sir
Thomas as a threat to his continued freedom and made up the
story of thieves ambushing them..."

Nicholas nodded, then turned to them. "The servants mentioned something about bandages on his head when he arrived
here. Perhaps to disguise his face somewhat? Or at least for a time
until he could replace the key household staff."

He turned to John again. "What really happened to my father
that day? Had you planned it all along or did you take advantage
of yet another opportunity?"

John fought to get out of the chair, but was held down in
Benjamin's grip. Still struggling, he aimed pleading eyes toward
Nicholas. "He was taking me to the constable and after all I suffered to avoid prison the first time, I couldn't do it again. I pan-
icked. I did what I had to do..."

Whatever else John might have said was drowned out by the
reaction of the crowd to his admission of murder.

But Nicholas was stuck on a different part of his confession. He
raised his voice. "What did you mean by avoiding prison the first
time? Is that how you came to join the Royal Navy?"

Another baronet stepped up and nudged his side. "Does this
scoundrel happen to hail from the Yorkshire Dales?"

Nearby, John grew even more frantic to escape while Benjamin laughed. "Aye, but that was all he'd tell us while Sir Nicholas here could not be kept quiet about this castle and his beloved valley."

The newcomer turned to the duke. "I hail from Leyburn and seem to recall that a John Marbury was arrested for suspicion of murder of his employer about three years ago but escaped from the jail leaving an unconscious jailer behind. A man who later died from his wounds."

John yanked hard against his restraints, veins bulging in his neck. "I was innocent but no one would believe me."

The duke raised a hand and silence fell over the room. "You expect us to believe a man who would go to such lengths—" He gestured to Nicholas and the castle at large. "—to save his own skin?"

He should pity the man, but in truth, only felt relieved that justice was inevitable. John would have to answer to the authorities for his own actions.

Middlesbrough turned to Nicholas. "Have you a dungeon here or should these fine men escort him to the village constable?"

Nicholas shrugged. "I cannot vouch for the security of such on these grounds as they have not been needed in centuries."

Laughter rippled through the room, until the duke turned to face the prisoner. "You, John Marbury, are hereby charged with at least three counts of murder both in Yorkshire and the London docks, in addition to the fraud and thievery you have perpetrated on the rightful baronet, his home, and his business holdings."

Nicholas glanced at a few of the unfamiliar faces in the room who seemed equally apologetic and horrified to have been deceived. He would have to mend those relationships. Later.

The duke nodded to Captain Drake and Benjamin. "Take him away and notify the magistrate that I recommend the harshest of all penalties post haste."

"Please, Sir Nicholas, have mercy." John was practically begging as the men pulled him out of the chair.

"You were once a friend, but now..." Nicholas shook his head as sorrow weighed heavy on his heart. "What you have done here was not an accident. May God have mercy on your soul but this matter is now out of my hands."

Others in the room parted to clear a path toward the door and Nicholas trailed behind them to where he had last seen Harold. "Please hitch a wagon immediately."

"Yes, my lord." His stablemaster and childhood companion spoke boldly as if glad to see him in authority. "I will see them safely to town."

"Thank you." He raised his voice. "And Benjamin?"

His crew mate glanced back over his shoulder from nearer the door. "Aye?"

"Hurry back with the captain, for we have much to catch up on."

Benjamin grunted. "We do. Not to mention, after years of enduring your stories, I still want to see this valley and castle of yours."

Nicholas could not help but smile.

God had certainly blessed him with the most loyal of companions.

Susannah's heart warmed to see Nicholas with his friends.

Now that his identity had been established and his inheritance reclaimed, an invisible burden seemed to have lifted from his shoulders. True, there was still grief over the loss of his father, but Nicholas truly belonged here among the well-dressed nobility and wealthy businessmen already stepping forward to greet him as he made his way back toward the duke.

While the last half hour had not gone according to plan, having everyone in the same room had hastened the outcome. She'd never been so proud of the way he handled himself.

Almost as if he had been born to the role.

A smile curved her lips.

He truly wore the Pennington name with honor.

"Your grace?" Nearby, the pleading voice of her stepmother sent chills up her spine.

She turned to see the woman had pulled Susan forward to stand before the duke with Pru right behind them.

"What justice is there for us? We honored the betrothal agreement in good faith and have been equally deceived."

Nicholas' battle might be over, but hers had just begun.

Keenly aware of the gaping guests around them, Susannah stepped toward the duke and lifted her chin. "There was *no* good faith demonstrated in substituting one bride for another."

How dare the woman claim innocence?

Susannah's fingernails bit into her palms as she glared at her stepmother.

The woman leaned toward the duke as if confiding a secret, but did not lower her voice. "Where is our justice? Even now my daughter could be with child—"

Susannah rolled her eyes. "You are the one who is a disgrace! I could have told you the man was false if you had only given me the chance."

She felt Nicholas' presence beside her and risked a quick glance, thankful for his support even as she knew she had to take the first step.

Now it was time to tell her story.

Susannah removed her apron in an attempt to appear less like a maid and turned to the frowning duke. "Your grace, it is a pleasure to see you again in this very same room."

The duke's forehead wrinkled as if he were trying to place her, his gaze darting from one young woman to the next.

"Do not let the garb foisted upon me deceive you. My father, Sir William Stanley, and I attended the celebration when Sir Thomas was awarded the baronetcy."

Susan pushed her way forward. "No. I was the one who attended at his side for he had not yet married Mama."

"Mama?" She raised an eyebrow. "You admit to your true relationship?"

"She gave me leave to call her thus since I had lost my own mother years before." Her stepsister widened her eyes in presumed innocence.

Tears pricked her eyes. Susan knew nothing about the former Lady Stanley or her loss. "You lie."

"Be silent." Her stepmother hissed. "Your father would be ashamed."

She sucked in a quick breath, reaching for the truth. "Yes, *my* father. And he would be proud of me. He wished for me to be kind to his new wife and her daughters, but not at this cost." She gestured to her clothing. "Not to be locked away in my room in Liverpool while you conspired to steal the only thing I had left from him. My betrothal to Nicholas."

Chapter Eighteen

Nicholas could not be prouder of Susannah for speaking the truth, but he'd been there abovestairs not an hour past when the vicious Lady Stanley had dared lay a hand on her.

His claim as the rightful baronet was aided by the testimony of others, and now it was time for him to step forward as a witness on her behalf.

He cleared his throat and addressed the duke. "Your grace, if I may be so bold, I would tell you the story of how my Susannah, the woman I love, came to have a scar on her forearm."

Pink blossomed on her face as Susannah turned her arm so the duke could see the jagged line running from wrist to elbow.

Her stepmother whirled toward him. "You know not of what you speak for by your own admission you have been out of the country."

"Her unfortunate injury happened *before* I left and years before *you* married the widowed knight." He smiled down into Susannah's eyes. "After all, the bedraggled child I rescued on the cliff above the waterfall was only there to mourn the recent loss of her mother while singing the most beautiful song."

"Singing?" Middlesbrough rocked on his heels. "I do recall the ceremony here and a lovely young girl on the cusp of womanhood."

The false Lady Pennington sashayed forward and preened in her finery. "It was I, your grace."

Susannah sucked in a quick breath, then lifted her chin. "If so, then delight us all with the melody you sang."

Her stepsister fluttered a hand over her bodice. "It has been so long that I cannot recall what festive tune I might have chosen."

Susannah took a step forward. "Come now. Certainly Reverend Brooks—our former vicar who is now a bishop in the Diocese of Carlile and who I spoke with just hours ago in Ravenglass—would recall the reason for specifically asking the real Miss Stanley to sing."

Ah, yes. They had another very credible witness nearby who would be familiar with all of the women.

With wide eyes and an opened mouth, the young woman edged backward behind her mother and glanced toward the exit...except her escape was blocked by the crowd who had pressed in further to eavesdrop.

Susannah turned toward the duke. "It was not a celebratory or festive tune, but rather a lament to honor the fallen as they protected our shores. A Scottish song I learned from my mother's lips."

The duke nodded slowly. "I do recall. Would you do me the honor...?"

"Yes, your grace." Susannah glanced at Nicholas and took a deep breath. "I've heard the lilting, at the yowe-milking, Lasses a-lilting before dawn o'day. But now they are moaning on ilka green loaning, the flowers of the forest are a' wede away."

Her voice was as sweet and pure as he remembered and a few bystanders murmured either in admiration or recollection or both. But too soon—as she closed her eyes and a single tear drifted down her cheek—the lyrics reminded him of all he had lost as well. And of all those who had not been as blessed to return home.

Including Stefan.

Having recalled the song many a time over the years, he joined her in singing the last stanza, just like she had taught him so many years before above the waterfall. "Sighing and moaning, on ilka green loaning. The flowers of the forest are all wede away."

The last notes lingered in the room followed by a hushed silence.

The flowers had withered, but it was possible for new ones to bloom.

"You have moved me to tears once again, Miss Stanley." The duke swiped at his face, then cleared his throat. "But how came you to be a maid? Even as a widow, surely the new Lady Stanley would not allow..." He gazed in confusion at the disparity of their clothing.

She looked to Nicholas and he nodded. "Speak the truth. All of it."

Susannah drew back her shoulders. "She more than allowed it, your grace. After years of housework in the guise of frugality while her daughters enjoyed elaborate debuts, she went so far as to forge indenture papers binding me to this castle." She ignored the gasps nearby and continued on. "And since I am not yet of age, she also threatened me with Bedlam if I tried to reveal the truth that her daughter Susan was not the same Susannah named in the betrothal agreement between my father and Sir Thomas."

A cold fury grew in the duke's eyes. "Are you saying there were not one, but two impostors exercising deceit upon each other and the community at large? The church will have to sort out the legalities of such a marriage. But you—" He turned his icy glare on her stepmother who cringed. "You knowingly facilitated the current fraud of a marriage while also depriving your husband's true daughter of her due. You are a disgrace to womanhood. Know this...I will be contacting the magistrates as well as the heir to Dalegarth about additional penalties."

The woman tugged on her daughters' arms while trying to back away.

He directed his next words to the false Lady Pennington. "And you...you were not forced to take any vows before God and therefore I hold that any resulting disgrace or consequence is yours alone to bear."

Susan's face paled considerably.

Middlesbrough looked to Nicholas. "I assume you wish them gone within the hour."

Nicholas nodded. "If not sooner."

The duke's lips twitched before he gestured for Nicholas to take charge.

Right. Because it was his role as lord of the castle.

Heat rushed up his neck as he called for the blatantly eavesdropping Mr. Ellis. "Reinstate Gibbs and Richards immediately and dismiss John's hires as we discussed. Have my housekeeper send someone to aid the packing so they do not take any of my mother's jewels with them. I'll allow a wagon transport to Ravenglass but no further."

Lady Stanley dragged a sputtering Susan toward the door with the younger sister trailing behind them. Once again, the path was clear as others in the room had stepped back in disgust.

"Well done, Sir Nicholas." Middlesbrough chuckled beside them. "I assume you and your betrothed will be hosting tonight's dinner?"

His betrothed?

Yes, they had been reinstated to their rightful places and it was time to celebrate.

Nicholas glanced down at Susannah's wide smile and then at the clock over the fireplace. "It may be a bit delayed, but yes." He looked around at the gathered guests. "The future Lady Pennington and I welcome you all to Muncaster Castle. I pray the remainder of your stay contains less drama than the past hour."

Laughter and smiles emerged all around as the awkward situation was brushed aside.

"We will meet on the morrow to discuss your placement on the Official Roll as baronet, but until then, I will retire before dinner." The duke excused himself and soon the room emptied.

Nicholas squeezed Susannah's elbow and turned to escort her out. "My lady, I suppose we too should dress for dinner."

She aimed a brilliant smile his direction. "Welcome home, Nicholas."

It was the same words she had spoken in the kitchen garden not so many weeks ago.

He could not contain the love swelling in his chest and leaned forward to bestow a kiss of promise, only to be interrupted by a clearing throat.

He jerked his head around to find Mr. Gibbs at hand.

The butler's eyes twinkled with unspoken laughter. "Sir Nicholas, Mr. Ellis and I have arranged for proper dinner garments for you. And before the evening is done, your belongings will be moved to the lord's chambers in place of the..." His face twisted in revulsion. "His presence will be rapidly removed."

"Thank you." As expected, the loyal servant was quickly setting the household to rights. However, his garments were not the only ones to consider. "Perhaps you should have Mrs. Richards claim a dress of Susan's before she leaves..."

Susannah tugged on his arm slightly. "I have one of my own that will be suitable for dinner and tonight's entertainment, however..." She turned her attention to the restored butler. "A few additional garments for the remainder of the house party would be appreciated."

"I will see that it is done, my lady." The butler bowed and scurried away.

There was none more suitable to fill the role of hostess by his side, and yet he equally loved the waterfall waif and the garden assistant.

If only their fathers could see them now.

If only they were alone and she was properly his wife.

Soon and very soon.

Susannah smoothed the burgundy fabric over her hips, thankful for the subdued style that allowed a ball gown to be deemed appropriate for a formal dinner.

And equally grateful for the indomitable Mrs. Richards who had ordered a bath to be drawn, someone to press the wrinkles from her dress, and another maid to style her hair.

It was a relief to know she would no longer need to deal with the stern Mrs. Finch or Mr. Morton. Instead, Mrs. Richards—like the cook Mrs. Jennings—had welcomed Susannah as if she was a long-lost daughter and was already making arrangements for a dressmaker and the transfer of her belongings abovestairs once the former occupant's suite was cleaned.

The servants' gossip spread fast and already she had received multiple apologies from those who had earlier believed her to be her stepsister's spy. Meanwhile, her roommate Edith scurried around with stars in her eyes, practically swooning over the romance of Susannah's childhood betrothal and eventual reunion with the rightful baronet.

Nicholas had sent word for her to join him near his rooms so they could make their entrance together. A proposal that left her slightly queasy with anticipation. She was eager to see him…and somewhat reluctant to be put on display.

However, since she was ready, rather than stewing in private, she opted for action. With a final glance at her attire, Susannah left her basement room and took the servant's stairs, stepping into the hall, not far from her new rooms.

God willing, her temporary rooms before she shared a suite with her husband.

Her face heated considerably at the thought of what being the future Lady Pennington entailed, even as she made her way down the hall.

She did not see a lingering footman in the area and was glad their guests were primarily housed in the other wing where they could not observe her embarrassed hesitation to answer Nicholas' summons.

Was she worthy of mingling among them as the wife of no-bility? Nicholas believed it so. As well as the former baronet. After all, she was born the daughter of a knight and not the maid the others saw in the drawing room earlier...

She straightened her shoulders and lifted her chin.

However, despite her bravado, she was still at a loss for the proper protocol when responding to a private summons. Should she knock on his door?

Somewhere down the hall, a clock chimed.

There were still fifteen minutes until they were to descend, but already a distant murmur of voices signaled that others were beginning to leave their rooms.

Ill at ease, she longed for Nicholas' stability. She raised a shaking hand to knock but the door opened before she could make contact.

There in the doorway stood the tall, wide-shouldered, well-dressed gentleman she had always imagined Nicholas to be, even with a growing bruise on his jaw from his earlier fight with John.

This was the man who conversed with dukes, earls, and naval officers as if he belonged. The man who had been born to the position and now dressed the part of country gentleman.

Except this version from her dreams was sweeping admiring eyes over her hair and gown. "You are a vision."

"I thank you, Sir Nicholas." She dropped into a quick curtsy only because it felt appropriate.

"None of that, my darling." He shook his head and joined her in the hallway. "Please call me Nicholas as you always have." His gaze drifted over her face and lingered on her lips. "Now that we seem to have so quickly settled the issues of our identities and my inheritance, all that remains is to make you my wife."

She struggled to draw a full breath, but knew exactly how he felt.

His eyes found hers. "We can have the banns read and be married by Midsummer's Eve if you so desire."

She could only manage a nod, then flushed at the decadent thought that this man would be hers. Her eyes swept over his profile.

Brown hair that was slightly tousled despite his recent grooming efforts and begging for her fingers to smooth it. A straight nose. Firm jawline and soft kissable lips that were curling into a smile.

"Soon, my love."

She lifted her gaze to see dark brown eyes brimming with promise. His appreciation ignited a new boldness and she winked. "So you say."

He chuckled and reached for her hand. "I do."

She grinned. "It is good that you are practicing your vows."

Heat flared in his eyes. "Life with you will never be dull."

She found it difficult to breathe. "I shall endeavor to make that so."

He lifted her hand to his lips and lingered there as her pulse tripped erratically in her wrist and their trapped gaze communicated a wealth of unspoken vows.

A noise down the hall had him releasing her hand, then turning slightly to offer his arm. "Shall we join our guests for dinner?"

She blushed again as she rested her hand on his sleeve.

However, as they made their way down the carpeted hall surrounded by centuries of history, doubts began to assail her. "Do I truly belong in a castle such as this among nobility? After all, I'm just a girl from Boot." She swallowed her pride. "A motherless ragamuffin—"

"Cease such foolish talk." He stopped their progress. "That girl captured my heart with her love of this valley and her devotion to her family." He pressed a hand over hers on his arm. "Your song and words of encouragement carried me through many a difficult time and I fear I cannot fulfill my father's expectations without you by my side."

She saw the doubt in his eyes. "You can. I know it. For not only were you born to this role in this—your home—but those years at sea shaped you into a capable leader."

Lines crossed his forehead as he frowned.

She placed her free hand atop the pile. "Not only has the staff yielded to your leadership over the past few weeks, but I saw how your captain and crew mate responded to you. And their admiration extended to the faces of the others."

"There is only one among the crowd who matters." His lips curved.

Her answering smile grew. "Are you begging more flattery, my lord?"

Nicholas' burst of laughter ended with a full smile as he resumed their journey toward the main staircase. "I believe we shall see who acquires the most admirers this evening as we celebrate God's victory in our lives."

Yes, there was much to celebrate.

Thank You, Almighty God, for justice.

Life had kept them apart for so many years—and there were still battles to be fought—but if they could survive thus far, with God's help they could overcome any future obstacle. Together.

Nicholas paused at the top of the stairs. "My dear, are you ready to be a baronetess and the mistress of this castle?"

She lifted her eyes to those of her future husband. "As long as we can occasionally explore our valley and bring its beauty here, it will seem like a glorious dream." She caught a quick breath at the overwhelming love in his eyes.

He brushed a kiss over her lips, followed by a whisper. "Like finding home."

You've finished this book, so what's next?

Want more castle stories?

If you missed any of the previous books in the series, you can find them at your favorite online retailer. (And do not fear, more historical novels are in the planning stages—so make sure to get on my email list to be notified when they are coming out!)

Or you can read on for a glimpse into the next book in my castle series: *Saving Grace*. Set in a castle in Colorado, this contemporary romance weaves elements of the previous four books into one.

Because not all heroes wear a uniform.

If you'd like to receive updates about upcoming books or sales, you can sign up for my email list on my website at CandeeFick.com.

(There might be a few surprises headed your way including a free novella and other exclusive bonus content.)

Dear Reader,

Thank you for spending a few hours of your time with me.

There is no greater pleasure as an author than knowing that I've encouraged my readers! If you enjoyed this book, please take a few minutes to let the rest of the world know by leaving a review at your favorite retailer or on sites like Goodreads or BookBub. It doesn't have to be long. Just a few words pointing other readers this direction would be much appreciated.

As I continue to write stories of faith, hope, and love, my prayer is that you will experience the amazing love of God and find encouragement for the journey called life.

Until we (hopefully) meet again in the pages of a book, happy reading everyone!

Candee

Preview: Saving Grace

Within the Castle Gates Book Five

Not all heroes wear a uniform.

Scarred as a teen in the accident that claimed her family, Grace
Thompson now volunteers as a guide at a Colorado castle. She
escapes her pain through the pages of a book while avoiding her
former guardian's pressure to pursue a stable teaching career. Until

the day a handsome soldier signs up for her tour and challenges her to stop living in other people's stories.

Drew Miller spent the last eight years teaching survival skills in the Air Force. But the needless death of a childhood friend has him re-examining the future since he can't seem to save the ones who matter most. He's there for a spiritual retreat, but spending time with Grace ignites the desire to chart a new course...even if it means leaving her behind.

At a crossroads, his personal mission to make a difference clashes with her need to please the only family she has left. With two hearts longing for a home, can love survive the inevitable distance?

This next installment of the Within the Castle Gates series weaves elements of the first four stories into a contemporary setting. If you like faith-based romance and rooting for the underdog, then you'll love .

Prologue

"Will you marry me?"

For the second time in minutes, there were not enough words to express her heart. But only one was needed. "Yes."

His answering gaze heated, and he lowered his smiling lips to hers. And then no words were needed at all.

Grace Thompson closed the book and hugged it to her chest. How she loved happy endings. Then again, what fifteen-year-old girl didn't?

She snuggled deeper into her favorite chair in the loft, soothed by the murmured voices of her parents through the adjacent door. Somewhere downstairs in the bunk room, her younger brothers were likely swapping gross jokes with the Howard boys and plotting their next adventure while Mrs. Howard rocked the baby to sleep in the master bedroom.

Once Mr. Howard arrived in the morning after a last-minute business meeting, their annual Spring Break vacation to the Howards' cabin would officially begin.

A smile curved her lips.

Her dad's old college roommate and his clan were practically family and while other people might swarm to the beaches for suntans, she much preferred the mountains and if she were lucky, snowshoeing through the pines to reach majestic views. Followed by hot chocolate beside a crackling fire, then curling up under a soft blanket to read a book.

If only the rest of her life could be this perfect.

After a sudden yawn about unhinged her jaw, she rose to her feet, set her book on the small table, and blew out the candle. Time to join the Howards' ten-year-old daughter on the pull-out sofa bed.

The tip of the still-hot wick glowed in the dark, but did not cast enough light to prevent her from knocking her leg against the corner of the table while stumbling her way to the railing. Something fell from the impact but it was too dark in the shadowed loft to see clearly.

Whatever it was, she'd have to pick it up in the morning.

Grace rubbed the sore spot on her thigh, then shuffled her feet across the wooden floor until she reached the top step. Between her past familiarity and the dim light from the kitchen's oven clock, she easily made her way down to the living room.

Minutes later, she was in her pajamas with freshly brushed teeth and tucked in beside Charity's warmth. As her eyes closed on the pillow, her mind drifted back to the story she'd just finished.

One day, she hoped God would send her a dreamy hero of her own.

Some time later, Grace awoke to a woman's scream, then curled up in a violent coughing fit, vaguely aware of heat, smoke, and a crackling sound. Almost like a...

Fire!

She burst upright and blinked away the tears filling her stinging eyes. Bright light came from the back half of the cabin as flames consumed the loft and crawled down the walls leading to the other bedrooms.

The loft where she'd sat just hours before reading by candlelight.

When she knocked against the table, had she...? No. It was unthinkable.

Another coughing fit stole her breath, then spurred her into action. She shook her bedmate awake, then ran toward the flames. "Mom! Dad!"

She had one foot on the bottom step when the loft's railing fell, breaking the top section of stairs loose in an explosion of sparks that cascaded down and ignited the rug beneath the dining table.

Her path upward was officially blocked. As was her parents' escape.

With a sob, Grace covered her mouth with her arm, then pivoted toward the other bedrooms and the spreading inferno. Through the thick red-tinted smoke filling the hall, she thought she saw a shadowy figure in a doorway before it slammed shut. Mrs.

Howard? But what about the—"Boys! Get up and break the window!" It was their only hope.

She sucked in a deep breath to yell again, but the overheated air scorched her lungs.

Dear God, please get them out!

Driven backward by the intense heat, Grace tripped over a chair and fell to the floor where the air was a bit easier to breathe. But from her new position, she spotted the flames already licking across the ceiling as the fire found new fuel and gained momentum.

There would be no saving the cabin with its thick beams and wood shingled roof.

Guilt clawed at her chest. Was it her fault?

Her parents didn't deserve such a fiery fate...nor did her brothers or any of the others.

She heard a keening wail behind her.

The least she could do was rescue someone.

Grace swallowed another sob, then crawled her way back toward the couch and the girl who was coughing hard enough to gag. What had those elementary school visits from firefighters said to do?

"Come on, Cherry." Grace forced the words out of a raw throat.

With a shaky hand, she pulled the girl down to the floor, then grabbed a T-shirt from her overnight bag beside the couch. After wrapping it around Charity's head to block even more of the smoke, she dragged the girl behind her toward the front door.

Why was she so weak?

Just feet from the exit, the roaring overhead was interrupted by an even-louder cracking sound. Some dormant reflex had Grace throwing her body over that of the girl, curling around her a moment before a crushing weight landed on her right shoulder, forcing the joint into an unnatural position. The agonizing impact was followed an instant later by searing pain and the scent of burning flesh and singed hair.

A scream ripped from her lips.

Beneath her, Cherry whimpered.

They had to get out before it was too late. Grace grit her teeth and tried to push up against the weight, but it was too much and darkness crept in on the fringes of her vision.

God, please...

A blessed numbness spread around her shoulder, but the scalding continued down her arm and across her back as the sizzling from the burning beam echoed too close to her ear.

"Help!" The shouted plea hurt her already-damaged throat. And then...

"Someone's inside!" A deep voice on the other side of the door sparked hope to life. "Call for help."

"Andy!" Another slightly-slurred voice joined the first. "You can't go in there."

"I have to."

The door opened and although the fresh oxygen fueled the flames, it cleared enough of the smoke that she was able to draw a fresh breath. She blinked through tear-filled eyes to see a large back-lit silhouette an instant before a flashlight blinded her vision.

"Help..." Her throat spasmed.

The flashlight landed near her face and then a hand touched her head. "I've got you."

"Save her." Her strength was failing, but at least the girl crying and wiggling in her arms had a fighting chance now.

Their rescuer gasped. "There's two of them."

The weight on her body lifted slightly, then the man—Andy—hissed as if he'd burned himself before the beam settled back into place, forcing the breath from her lungs.

Yea though I walk through the valley of the shadow of death...

"Dear Jesus... Help us..."

"You did your part, now let me do mine." She was vaguely aware of him whipping off his shirt and wrapping his hands in the fabric. "When I lift, can you try to crawl forward?"

She nodded. Time was running out and they only had one chance.

God, give me strength...

She drew her legs up, bare toes catching on the rough floor and bracing to push them toward freedom.

He counted down from three, then after a grunt, the weight on her back shifted again.

This time, she let the adrenaline flooding her veins empower a final surge as she scrambled toward the door, dragging Charity along with her.

Moments later, she was lifted in strong arms and carried into the dark night.

"You're safe now."

And then the world went black.

Get the rest of *Saving Grace* today.

More Fiction

A complete and up-to-date list of all my books can be found on my website at CandeeFick.com

Standalone Romance

Catch of a Lifetime (Cassie and Reed)

The Wardrobe Series

(Contemporary romance in theater settings)
Dance Over Me (Dani and Alex)
Focus on Love (Liz and Ryan)

Sing a New Song (Gloria and Nick)
A Picture Perfect Christmas (Liz and Ryan continued)
Home For Christmas (Grace and Tyler)
Complete Series Boxed Set

Within the Castle Gates Series

(Historical romance in various time periods)
Stepping Into the Light (Moira and Evan)
To Win Her Heart (Emma and Grayson)
The Lost Heir (Kathleen and Reuben)
Finding Home (Susannah and Nicholas)
Saving Grace (contemporary - Grace and Drew)
A Castle in the Clouds (Miranda and Josh)
Books 1-4 Boxed Set

About Candee

C andee Fick is a multipublished, award-winning author. She is also the wife of a high school football coach and the mother of three children, including a daughter with a rare genetic syndrome. When not busy writing, editing, or coaching other authors, she can be found exploring the great Colorado outdoors, indulging in dark chocolate, and savoring happily-ever-after endings through a good book.

Visit her website at CandeeFick.com where you can find out about her latest releases and sign up for her email list.

www.ingramcontent.com/pod-product-compliance
Lightning Source LLC
Chambersburg PA
CBHW022012170626
46808CB00001B/370